# WILD VIOLET

## BY

## ARIEL C. HORN

# WILD VIOLET

*Dedicated to my ancestors, whose courage, tenacity, and devotion inspired me to write this story.*

# Texas: 1869

# Chapter I

Violet's spurs jingled as she walked across the wooden floor. All heads turned to see the stranger who had entered the saloon. To their surprise the stranger was a woman. She was wearing a man's shirt and trousers. She packed an ivory-handled pistol. The men stared slack-jawed. The spittoon rang in the silence from a single chaw of tobacco. The woman-stranger sat herself down at the corner table. The Black Dog saloon was the only place in town where anyone could get a drink and some hot grub for supper. The bartender was drawn out from behind the bar to ask the lady what she wanted.

She answered, "Sarsaparilla, and—"

Derisive laughter erupted from some of the men at the bar. A tall man stood up and twisted his dark, unkempt beard. He was a hulking mass. His scaly lips spread across his grimy teeth and formed into a mocking smile. He walked a step forward and spat tobacco on the floor.

"Hey!" he shouted at her in a brusque, gravelly voice. He was drunk. "How much?"

Violet's throat went dry, she was afraid to even answer. Swift rage swept across his face.

"Hey! I asked you a question, whore! How much for one night?" he shouted.

She sat there in stunned silence, her hat covering her eyes.

"I ain't no whore," she said.

The tall man spat the rest of his chaw on the floor.

"What do you mean you ain't no whore?" he slurred, "If I call you one then you are!" He issued a drunken laugh, which the many men at the bar echoed.

"I ain't," she said as calmly and as quietly as the first time. The big man lumbered towards her. Her hand was solid on the grip of her pistol. She silently pulled back the hammer half-cocked under the table.

A cowboy sat up from the bar and grabbed the tall man's arm from behind, causing the tall man to spin around. The cowboy pulled his right arm back and punched the tall man straight on the chin. The tall man staggered back and then fell with a loud thud on the floor.

"She said she ain't no whore." The cowboy said with a soft drawl.

The tall man drunkenly stumbled back onto his feet, and using his momentum he took a swing at the cowboy that was reminiscent of a grizzly bear swatting at his prey. The too-powerful force of the swing caused him to tip forward. The cowboy punched him with a left deeply in the gut and took his right knee and planted it in the tall man's forehead, which almost knocked the big man down to the ground, but he regained his footing. The big man gritted his teeth as he addressed the men at the bar, "Ain't any of you cowards gonna do somethin'?"

"Good luck Jasper." An anonymous voice called from the background.

Jasper lunged forward and managed to punch the cowboy on the jaw. The cowboy shook his head and quickly recovered, coming back with a right to Jasper's jaw.

"What the hell are you doing, punk? Don't you know who I am?" The tall man screamed from a swollen mouth.

"Sure do, pard."

The cowboy jibed from the left and then punched Jasper with a strong upper-cut to the chin. The big man fell into some empty chairs and splintered a table in two with a boisterous crash. The cowboy turned around and began to walk away, thinking that his job was done. Jasper lunged behind him with terrible speed, wrapped his arm around his neck, putting the cowboy in a headlock. The cowboy struggled to get free from his grasp, but Jasper's massive size and strength overtook him. He squeezed tighter around the cowboy's neck, cutting off his air supply. The cowboy's fingers slackened their grip on Jasper's burly forearm, and his face turned a blue shade of pale. Violet walked up behind them and raised her gun up high and pistol-whipped Jasper on the back of his head. The death grip he had on the cowboy loosened, and he fell to the ground like a gigantic sack of potatoes. He was licked, on the floor and humiliated, but still barely conscious. The cowboy coughed and rubbed his neck and breathed deeply as he tried to recover. He looked at the woman-stranger with a mixture of perplexity and amazement. She seized the opportunity to get out quickly before Jasper got off the ground and realized what had happened.

Billy bounded out of the saloon, hoping to follow her. The mysterious woman had already untied her horse and was ready to mount her painted mustang. He noticed a hint of hurt and tears in her dark eyes—a stark contrast with her tough outer image.

As she looked down at him from her horse the man's blue eyes softened. She surmised the cowboy was fairly young, probably in his early twenties. He had a good-sized rounded jaw and an ingenuous face. He had a medium build. She noticed his well-built forearms were clad in star studded leather cuffs.

"Thank you," she said, "I'm sorry about what happened in there."

"I'm sorry about that too ma'am—I don't know what gets into some men." he said.

"Whiskey," she said.

She kicked her horse and she went off on a gallop. The saloon doors creaked open followed by the uneven, thudding, footsteps of Jasper. Blood dripped from his swollen lower lip as hatred and rage gleamed in his eyes. He watched the woman on the painted mustang ride out of town.

Billy was in the saddle as Jasper fired a shot in his direction, but he missed and obliterated a shop window. Two other men joined their friend from the alleyways adjacent to the saloon. They fired several more badly-aimed shots at Billy as he rode out low on his horse.

Billy knew that Jasper and his gang were going to try to kill him. He didn't want to think about the things that they might do to the girl if they got their hands on her. He knew that getting pistol-whipped by a woman was the final blow to

Jasper's pride, and that he wasn't the kind, forgiving sort. He had to warn her of the danger to her life.

The freshly disturbed dust indicated that she had ridden towards the northwest. With a loud yell and hard kick he forced his quarter horse on a fierce gallop. He knew that he could get good time on a group of drunken men, but he didn't want to take any chances. They were still dangerous and their horses could still carry them. He was going to have the hardest time catching up to the girl on the little mustang.

* * *

Violet rode hard. She sought solace in speed. She wanted to leave that town behind her. All she had wanted to do at the saloon was to get a drink and some grub to eat, not to incite a bar fight.

Perhaps she would sleep out. She couldn't get a hotel room like she had planned, although she hadn't slept in a real bed in weeks. The countryside swept out wide and gold, prickly pear dotting the landscape. She thought about the town she'd just departed. She disliked most towns; they were small, cramped boxes full of people. The prairie was the opposite, wide, wild and free. Here she would not be burdened with the troubles of the world.

She sensed a presence and could hear the faint sound of hooves beating in the distance. She turned her head to discover she was not alone. Behind her she could see a small cloud of dust coming up the trail and a man on a dark horse. She thought it might be one of the men from town, and that frightened her. Who he was, or why she was being followed she didn't know. She just didn't like it.

"Hyaw!" she yelled. The sturdy mustang breathed harder as she led it up a fork in the trail over a grassy hill.

\* \* \*

Billy forced his horse to go even faster when he saw her disappear over the horizon. If he rode away from the girl, he might steer them away from her. But which prey would they follow? Something about the look in Jasper's evil eyes made him know that he would exact revenge on the both of them. Jasper never let his women get away. He knew this from talk around town that many a woman's virtue had been sullied by Jasper. A lesser man would've regretted the decision to stop him, but Billy didn't. Still, chivalry wasn't always rewarded.

* * *

Violet slowed her horse to a trot, and listened, hoping she would no longer hear the hoofbeats of the horse that had been following her. Soon she realized that same rider was barreling up behind her. She kicked her horse, and the pinto went even faster. The pursuer had almost gained up to her. The chase was on, and soon both riders were at a full gallop.

Sweat dripped down her face as fear entered her heart. Her pursuer might be the man she pistol-whipped in the saloon. She looked back. He didn't seem as big as Jasper, but she couldn't be sure because his hat was blocking his face.

"Hey!" The voice yelled out in desperation. It sounded familiar. She slowed her horse down and turned around to face him, whoever he was, with her pistol drawn and cocked. The cowboy made a sudden stop. Her pistol was pointed right between his eyes.

He was the man who had defended her. She eased the hammer back and let the gun slide back into her holster. She was surprised to see him there. He looked almost embarrassed and flustered as he stared at the girl.

"I've come to warn you that those men will be looking for you." He gulped air since he was out of breath, "they're after me too."

"Alright," she said, "do you know where they are?"

"They're coming up from the southeast," he said as he motioned toward that direction with his head, "they'll be here soon, come on!"

His horse darted forward and he motioned her with his hand to follow. He led her up a rocky trail through some grassy hills. From near the top of a hill, they could see Jasper and his followers in the valley. They rode quickly around a series of knolls.

Violet wondered if she could trust the cowboy, so far he had done nothing but earn her trust. He had done what most men wouldn't have, and more. What did he have to gain from this? Perhaps if they worked together they would have a better chance of defending themselves. The horses were still panting hard after their intense gallop. She followed the stranger down a series of steep trails leading into a small canyon. The walls were steep, and the trails thin—better fit for a burro than a horse. She noticed an opening in the canyon wall. He made a left into the mouth of a cave big enough for the horses. He dismounted, and patted his horse with loving approval.

The cave looked like it had been occupied before; it exhibited an old fire ring, stacked firewood and some old cans. She dismounted when she got a bearing on her surroundings. Her horse was wet with sweat from the chase. The cowboy started to gather brush and other debris to place in front of the entrance to disguise their presence.

The cowboy had a fleeting smile, "This is where I used to go as a kid. No one else knows where this is." he said with quiet confidence as he tied up his horse to a dead juniper tree clinging to the rock.

Violet sat down on a large rock and took off her hat. Her light brown hair that had been bundled up under the crown of her hat flowed gracefully down her back. Her dark eyes cut like obsidian. They were like deep pools that reflected the stars at night. They were a rounded almond shaped that slanted upwards, framed by dark eyelashes. She had a wide face with high cheekbones, a rounded chin and a large jaw. There also seemed to be the impressions of dimples on her cheeks, which would be revealed if she ever smiled. There was a balanced mixture of strength and delicacy in her features.

"Who are you?" she asked the stranger, still a bit puzzled. The cowboy once again seemed a little embarrassed and taken off-guard.

"My name is William Colton. Most people call me Billy."

He put his hand out in preparation for a handshake. Violet cautiously reciprocated the gesture.

"I'm Violet." she said, and then stared at the ground.

He tried to break the awkward silence. "What brings you to these parts?"

She met his question with a cold, hard stare, and she answered defensively, "I was just trying to pass through. You?"

Billy continued to tend to his horse. "I live here. I'm a ranch hand for my father."

She wanted to ask him so many questions, like why he had helped her and was continuing to do so, but her reserved nature restrained her. Above the canyon the sound of horses could be heard disturbing loose rocks on the trail. Both occupants of the cave held their breath. Their horses' ears nervously twitched.

"Where the hell did they go?" a man shouted, the sound was muffled by the layer of rock. Billy put his hand on his horse to keep her quiet. The horses above them were making circles. The two figures in the cave stood stock still. Jasper announced to his compadres, "I'm going to find the son of a bitch, and that whore too."

They heard the horses gallop back towards town. Billy let out a long sigh from holding his breath. Violet looked perplexed.

"Who are they?" she asked.

Billy looked back at her—surprised she didn't know.

"His name is Jasper Smith. He doesn't like it when people get in his way." he paused as he looked up at the cave ceiling. "His brother is James Smith. They own a gold mine a few miles west of here, and pretty much the rest of the town, and a big ranch to boot. James is the brains of the outfit. Jasper thinks he can do whatever the hell he wants, and he gets away with it too... most of the time. He's no good rotten scum."

"Why did you fight him, and why did you choose to help me?" Her clear voice expressed genuine curiosity.

He answered quickly, "'Cause it was right. Somebody had to stand up to that bastard. Pardon my French, ma'am."

Violet looked up, surprised. "Not a lot of people do the right thing anymore."

He flashed a brief smile. "Jasper and his men will still be looking for you. You could come stay at my ranch for a spell—just until this whole thing blows over."

Violet was taken aback. "What about you? You're the one who did most of the licking; surely he's going to look for you too."

"It'll be alright. My Pa, Gustavo, and I can hold 'em off." The cowboy seemed overly confident.

"Hold on a minute," Violet interjected, "We don't need to bring your family into this, you've done enough!"

Billy's eyes grew sad. She realized she had hurt his pride. She touched his hand—the rough and calloused hands of a cowboy. She softened the tone of her voice, "I appreciate what you have done for me. I don't know what else you can do."

She took ahold of the reins of her mustang and walked out of the cave.

Billy watched her and her horse's silhouette against the sunset. His actions in the saloon protected her honor, and incidentally the life of a man (although he may have deserved the bullet).

Violet figured it was illogical for him to be involved further with her. She needed to be on her way anyway. What was the true threat of the drunkards? Her pony could outride them any day. She back-tracked, perhaps she was underestimating them. They didn't seem like the types to easily forgive a good licking and public humiliation. Maybe she really was in danger. But she was unused to receiving unsolicited help from strangers. She was unsure of what to do, so she did what she always did. Ride on. When she reached the top of the canyon she saw no sign of Jasper or his men. They could be back in town getting supplies and reinforcements for all she knew, or they could be languishing in their drunkenness. Jasper's money and connections frightened her more than anything. She didn't want to start a blood-feud between the Smiths and the Coltons, and she didn't want an enemy that had the means to chase her clear across Texas. She continued northwest, trying to leave the whole thing behind her. She heard someone following her. She drew her gun. It was Billy. His blue eyes were staring back at her, the size of saucers.

"Why do you keep doing that?" she said, slightly peeved. She holstered her gun.

"I wanted to give you an escort out of town." he said, "I figured you could use the extra gun."

"I can take care of myself," she huffed.

"They won't stop until they find you." His eyes were deeply intense with fear for her safety.

"What about you?" she asked.

Billy nodded in the affirmative.

"Where are you headed?" he asked.

"San Angelo." she said. Her eyes were focused on the horizon. Billy's eyebrows rose in surprise—maybe he had never been that far, well, neither had Violet.

"I'll ride with you to San Angelo." he spoke as if it were written in stone.

She questioned, "Do I have a choice?" He just grinned. She answered her own question with a frown, "I guess not."

She started her horse on a trot. Maybe this would work out after all: she could keep Billy away from town until Jasper sleeps off his drunkenness and forgets that anything ever happened. Maybe she would even lose her new compadre before she reached her final destination.

* * *

Billy had never seen a woman like her, strong and almost completely independent. He was almost intimidated yet intrigued by her. Why was she dressed like a cowpoke and traveling alone? The mystery raced through his mind like bees buzzing around a hive. He needed to get her away from town. He knew how powerful a man Jasper was, and how many allies he had. The whole town was practically under Jasper Smith's big dirty thumb.

Why was he accompanying her? Was it pride, foolishness, or for her own protection? All he knew is that he was driven by some unknown force.

# Chapter II

Darkness had fallen. Billy and Violet had been riding ever since they left the shelter of the cave. Violet stopped. She unbuckled the cinch of her saddle, and the whole thing was removed with lightning speed.

"What, are we stopping now?" Billy asked.

"Do you have any objections? Or do you think they aren't gonna sleep off those hangovers?"

Billy shrugged his wide shoulders. Violet laid out her bedroll.

"The moon is full. We don't need a fire." she ordered.

Billy agreed. The sky was a beautiful purple-blue and was dotted with stars. He took off his saddle and sat down on it. He felt uncomfortable—he was not used to being alone with a woman, especially since this one was a stranger.

"So..." was his valiant effort to make conversation. He spoke in a thick drawl. "Where're you from?" He hoped that question was innocent enough.

Home. She hadn't thought of it in a while. The quiet rolling hills, the horses and the log cabin came to her mind. She thought of all that she had left behind. All of those memories, like dark shadows, all linked to one place.

"Missouri." Her eyes seemed far away.

Billy waited a minute before he spoke, "I've lived here in Mustang Ridge all my life. Never knew any other place." He felt a certain loneliness for the mysterious stranger. Suddenly awkward, he searched for something else to say. "What brings you to Texas? Missouri is awful distant."

That was another difficult question for her to answer. He seemed to be more trouble than he was worth—just with these darned questions. She kicked off her worn leather riding boots. Billy waited for her answer, with a lack of response Violet indicated that was enough conversation for one night.

"That," she said as she crawled into her bedroll, "is a story for another time."

She was used to traveling alone, and his presence was disruptive compared to her usual solitude. She did not know what to make of him, and couldn't decide why he was sticking with her.

Billy got into his bedroll, clearly frustrated at the lack of cordial cooperation from the stranger. He watched her fall asleep contentedly, her hat covering her eyes.

He worried about Smith and his posse. They were also close to Indian lands. He struggled to stay awake, opening and closing his eyes, but he was unable to shake the feeling that a threat loomed around the corner. Soon slumber overtook him and he fell into a deep sleep.

\* \* \*

Billy woke up with a start. The golden light was shining on the prairie. Violet's bedroll was empty. Where had she gone? He felt all of a sudden that she might be in danger. He looked up and saw her standing about six feet away. She was wearing a buckskin vest and moccasins, and looked altogether like an Indian. She concentrated intently on the horizon. He tried getting up but she put out her hand as if to stop him. He stayed down. A single silhouette of a horseman appeared on the crest of a hill to the north.

"Don't make any sudden movements." she said as she untied her horse.

"Comanche?" he asked as he hurriedly pulled on his boots. He had heard tales of whole families getting scalped.

"No, Apache. He's a scout." she said.

"What difference does it make? They're both Indians."

"Enough of one," she rebuked him with a tight jaw and continued. "There may be others. If we get out of here quickly, and quietly we may be alright."

They mounted their horses and slowly started riding out of the valley. Billy's eyes darted about and sweat beaded on his brow. Another rider appeared on the crest of the hill to the south, and another. Two more riders joined the original on the north hill.

"We're surrounded." Billy said.

"Not quite, just keep moving."

Billy's horse neighed and jumped. All five of the riders rode down the hill into the valley, shouting as they went. The warriors encircled the two riders. They were all fierce, with red paint on their faces and feathers on their spears. The first rider, possibly the war chief, spoke first. His face was a deep russet and lined with a battlefield of wrinkles. He held his shoulders back in a proud and dignified manner. "Ya Ta Say... Deyaa." he addressed the girl.

Violet responded, "Ya Ta Say." She spoke a few more words in the language Billy could not understand. There was a younger Apache on the right side of the chief. He did not seem to trust the strangers as much as his leader.

The young warrior spoke under his breath angrily, "Netdahe!"

The chief raised his hand to silence him, and let Violet continue to speak. The chief raised an eyebrow at Billy, but seemed to respect, or at least tolerate Violet. After a few more words and gestures his once fierce face turned to peace. "Inju. Ka Dish Day" the chief said respectfully with a wave of his hand.

"Ashoge. Yadalanh." Violet responded. The chief signaled his party to depart. The young warrior was still suspicious of the strangers, especially Billy. His eyebrows slanted above his fiery black eyes. The party left just as quickly as they had appeared, except the young warrior. He still faced the strangers.

"Don't react," Violet cautioned.

As she and Billy were riding away the young warrior rode up with great speed to Billy and hit him hard on the shoulder with his bare hand. The young warrior rode away, yelling at his victory. Once he rejoined the party the chief stopped on the hill and looked back at them and rode away.

Billy sat still on his horse and was incredibly tense. "What the hell was that?"

"That's counting coup."

He looked back. "Why didn't he just kill me?"

"He didn't have to." she said.

After a few minutes Billy could speak again, "What on earth did you say to the chief back there?" He was shocked, surprised, and relieved all at the same time.

"Apache," Violet said with a smirk. She rode off ahead of Billy. He was still staring perplexingly into the distance at the Indian riders, and then to Violet. He made his horse turn to follow her.

"I don't think we'll have to worry about Jasper Smith too much." she said.

"Why is that?"

"Turns out the Chief has a score to settle with Jasper." she said, "I told him that he had been following us. Things might turn out just fine."

\* \* \*

Their horses trotted along for a few moments. Billy looked contemplative. "I should tell my Ma and Pa where I'm going before we go any further. They really depend on me on the ranch. It wouldn't hurt for us to pick up some supplies neither."

Violet smiled. "Now, you're not thinking of hunkering me down, are you?"

"It shouldn't have to come to that." Billy turned his horse around to the south and Violet followed. "It's actually not too far from here." he stated.

They rode in a southerly direction until Violet saw the house from the top of the hill. It was a good-sized one story log home hewn from live oak. A large kitchen garden spread out from behind the house. A few fruit trees stood in a grove. There were several outbuildings from the same construction as the house. Live oak trees with sprawling crowns surrounded the main property.

"Is that your home?" she asked with a quaver in her voice.

"Yep," Billy responded.

They rode down into the valley. Billy tied up his dark horse on a hitching post next to the stable.

"You stay here. I'm going to try to talk to my Pa and rustle up some vittles."

Violet did as she was asked, it was only polite. She hadn't seen a home like his over a month and it made her heart ache to imagine what might happen if Jasper and his gang came riding in with guns blazing. She stared at her boots as she waited for Billy.

"Hi." She heard a little voice behind her that surprised her and she spun around on her heel. There stood a little boy of about six years old. "What's your name?" he asked.

"Violet. What's yours?"

"My name is Cody." He paused and looked up at her. "What are you doing here?"

"Well... I'm..." She didn't really know how to explain the situation to the little boy.

"Do you know Billy?" he asked.

She felt a little relieved that she actually knew how to answer the question. "Yes, yes I do."

"Oh." He had a mischievous little grin on his face, "Is he your beau?"

"What? No!"

* * *

Billy found a small scrap of paper and managed to scribble out a note to his Pa in pencil explaining the situation as best he could. He found his mother in the kitchen, scrubbing the counter.

"Howdy Ma,"

She turned around and her weary eyes widened. "Where have you been? I've been worried sick about you! I had half a mind to have your Pa go after you himself! Thought you might be lying face-down in the mud with none of your wits about you, the way you've been hanging around those saloons as of late. It ain't healthy William Henry Colton!" She grabbed a wooden spoon and slammed it down on the counter with a loud clap.

Billy wasn't frightened by much, but one thing that could strike fear into his heart was his mother's wrath.

"You know I went to town for a job..." He tried to soften her anger.

"I know honey, but I'm worried about you hanging around the wrong places." She turned back to work at the counter. "Glad to see you back in one piece."

"Where's Pa?" Billy continued.

"He and Gustavo are rounding up some strays. What fer?" Billy handed his mother the small piece of paper. "What's this?"

"It's a note to Pa. I'm fixin' to be gone for a spell."

"What are you doing, Billy?" His mother worriedly demanded.

"A lady needs my help." He gestured to Violet outside talking to Cody.

"You're not in any trouble, now?"

"I got into a tussle with Jasper Smith."

"What in tarnation are you doing that fer?" His mother reprimanded him, "You know he and his brother are the most powerful men in three counties."

He looked out at Violet, "She needed protection from him. I need to get her out of town..." he paused before telling his mother the whole truth, "they're looking for me, I don't want them coming here to the ranch. Get Gustavo and the hands out to the perimeter."

Her son was a grown man, and must make his own decisions. She glanced out the window to Violet talking to her son Cody, and then looked back at Billy. "I reckon you'll be alright. Don't do anything foolish… ya hear?"

"I was hoping I could get some vittles for the road."

"That's right," His mother did a rapid search through the cupboards and grabbed several sacks and placed them in his arms. She pulled a tin of biscuits from the top shelf. "Here you go Billy. I know these are your favorites." She smiled and embraced her son. She watched through the teary eyes of a mother as he walked out the front door.

* * *

Violet heard Billy's footsteps on the front porch. She blushed red. Cody ran off giggling behind the house.

"I think I just met your little brother." she said, slightly annoyed.

Billy replied with a chuckle, "Oh! Cody? He's a hoot. My Pa isn't here. I left a note with my Ma for him, wrote in it that I wouldn't be back for a few weeks." Violet turned around, almost recovered. He was carrying what looked like a load of foodstuffs. "I picked up some flour, beans, jerky, coffee, and some biscuits." he said, "My saddlebags are in the stable."

He started walking toward the rustic looking building. She followed in after him. She attempted one more effort to dissuade him. "Are you sure you want to do this?" she said softly as she looked him in the eyes. Billy grabbed a large loop of rope and threw it over his shoulder. He gave her one glance, and she knew it would be near impossible to stop him. "San Angelo is a long way." she said, still trying to make a last ditch effort.

"I know." he said as he tied the lariat to his rig.

"Why do you want to help me?" Violet asked, this time a little desperate for an answer.

"I told you why, it's the right thing to do." he said, his voice sincere and gentle. "It's dangerous for a woman to travel alone, especially out here."

"I've been able to make it just fine until now."

"Listen, I'll ride with you to San Angelo, and then I promise I'll be out of your hair. I'm already up to my neck as it is."

Violet hung her head. She was being selfish, she forgot for a moment that Billy was also being chased by Jasper Smith.

"I'm sorry. It's your decision." She glanced at her horse. "Come on, let's get going." She half-smiled with reluctant anticipation.

No sooner were they on their horses than Cody jumped out from behind the side of the house and started waving frantically. "Bye Billy!" he said.

"I'll see you in a couple weeks Cody." Billy said, "Look after Ma and Junie, okay?"

The little boy smiled brightly. "Okay, I promise! Goodbye pretty lady!" Cody said.

Billy blushed, and turned his face away from his lady compadre, although Violet was amused.

"Bye Cody." she said.

"I told you he was a hoot." Billy then quietly said under his breath as they rode away, "I hope they'll be alright…"

# Chapter III

Billy and Violet continued to ride over the vast and lonesome Texas prairie. The noon sun shone high and bright in the sky. They had been riding for so long without the thought of eating. Billy's stomach growled.

"Hey, why don't we stop and rest a spell?" he suggested, "I'm sure the horses won't mind." His charming smile disarmed Violet.

"I wouldn't mind either," Violet replied, "I haven't eaten anything since before I rode through town. My dinner plans were a little spoiled." She winked—it was like a bit of warmth from a stone. Billy jumped off his saddle and tied their horses near a little grove of live oak trees. It was a small island of trees in a sea of rolling prairie. He started gathering sticks for firewood. There was a small creek running near the trees. Violet sat down on a large limestone rock. She hadn't realized how tired and hungry she was until her body was at rest. Her bones ached from riding so long. She just wondered how tired the horses must feel. The horses nibbled on the fleshy bits of green grass along the side of the creek, and quenched their enormous thirst with the clear water.

As Billy gathered firewood Violet desired to make herself useful. She was not one to rest long. She stumbled back up to search for a percolator from one of Billy's saddlebags. She hadn't had fresh coffee in a long time. As she searched through his belongings to find the coffee pot she had a sense she was invading something very personal. There was a large Bowie knife, with the initials W.H.C. carved into the leather sheath, a few candles, and a box of matches, a well-worn harmonica, a faded blue bandana, and a letter. She was tempted to open it, but she rejected the lightning quick impulse. She finally found the dented percolator at the bottom of the bag. She grabbed a sack of ground coffee, and the box of matches. She went to the creek to collect some clear water.

She watched Billy in the distance. Violet hadn't had the time to realize how attractive he was until now. He was taller than she had first suspected. His grey and brown checkered wool pants covered his muscular legs, his gun belt hung on his slender hips. Her eyes followed the length of his torso which was clad in his home-spun dark red shirt, all the way up to his broad square shoulders. She quickly turned her head, as a slight blush came to her cheeks. She couldn't allow herself to become too attached.

He returned with two handfuls of twigs.

"It's not much, but it should get the fire started." He set the tinder up in a tipi shape.

"I thought we might have some fresh coffee." Violet said as she held up the percolator.

"That sounds mighty fine." Billy said as he rubbed the back of his neck with his hand. The little fire started crackling. He retrieved some larger sticks from below the oak trees, and added them to the fire. He retrieved a grill grate from his other saddlebag, and set it out over the small but healthy blaze. He sat on the ground with a sigh and started to stare intently into the flames. Violet was tempted to ask him what he was thinking about, but decided to watch him in silence. Soon the coffee was ready.

Billy started making some beans, and grabbed a small tin of biscuits.

"Would you like one?" He offered.

Violet grabbed the tin and opened it. The hearty smell of flour and butter escaped.

"Much obliged."

She ravenously devoured a biscuit and handed the tin back to Billy. The dry biscuit hit her stomach like a small brick. She washed it down with a swig of coffee. The warmth of the hot drink sliding down her throat was soothing. The smell of beans was thick, and she waited in hungry anticipation.

"Have you ever been to San Angelo?" She tried to make her question sound casual and not judgmental. She wasn't sure if it worked.

"No." he replied, "but I'm purt'near sure how to get there." He paused for a moment and stared into the fire. "Why do you need to go to San Angelo?" he asked the question as if it had been clawing to get out. Violet was taken aback, and she was unsure of how to respond. The last few weeks had been a tempest of activity.

"It's personal business." She hoped it would satisfy his curiosity for the time being.

He looked at her hard for a moment and then went back to stirring the beans. "I hope you'll be willin' to tell me in time."

Violet was unsure of how to handle this situation. This young man had already risked his life for her, and had offered to travel with her far away from his family and responsibilities. She felt like she was selling him short. Violet always held her cards close to her vest. Concealing certain truths had become second nature to her. Sometimes it was a necessity.

She changed the subject, "How many brothers and sisters do you have?"

"Well, you met Cody back there, he's the youngest. Then there's Junie, she's my little sister. She's going on about twelve. Then there's my brother Paul, he's sixteen." His shoulders seemed to sink under the responsibility of being the oldest. "Beans are ready." he said.

Violet scooped a red pile onto her plate. She looked up and saw a dark horse with a rider on the horizon.

"Billy…" she said, alarmed. Her fork slipped out of her fingers and dropped with a clang onto her plate. Billy stumbled onto his feet. He hurried to his horse and grabbed his Henry rifle out of its leather sheath. Violet's small hand clutched the ivory grip of her revolver. She pulled back the hammer. There were three or four more riders behind the first.

"I can't tell who they are," Billy said, "they're too far away." He set up behind one of the larger oak trees. "At least we have cover."

Violet went behind the rock she had been sitting on. This was one of those times when she wished she had a long-range weapon. The riders pressed on, and it became apparent that one of them was Jasper Smith.

"Oh shit…" Billy breathed out slowly.

"I can't believe they followed us." Violet said breathlessly. She worried about being out-gunned by five people. Billy seemed to know what he was doing. She knew how to handle her gun, at least. However it would be a while until she would be able to get a shot off on any one of them. Violet recalled the meeting with the Apache earlier that morning.

The riders came closer and closer. They should have already made it into their range. Sweat beaded on Billy's brow, which he wiped away with his bandana. The riders stopped. A man with a top hat rode out from behind the others, volunteering himself as their spokesman.

"We see you over there!" he said in a high and raspy voice. "Just give us the girl, and we may pardon your sins Billy Colton!" He acted like an M.C. at a circus. He paused for dramatic emphasis. "Either that or we'll shoot you out like rats!"

Violet shouted back, "This *girl* ain't going nowhere with the likes of you!"

Billy replied, a little caught-off-guard, "Th-That's right! We don't want to cause you any more trouble. Y'all better ride on outta here, and you may be spared." he said, with as much bravado as he could muster. The man in the top hat laughed a raspy, throaty laugh. It was followed by chuckles from the rest of the group, except for Jasper who sat like a colossal statue atop his horse.

The man in the top hat suddenly crumpled forward in his saddle, stuck by an arrow in his back. There was the sound of horses neighing from the urgent orders of their masters, metal coming out of oiled holsters, and the nearly simultaneous clicks of gun hammers being pulled back. About a dozen Apache rode screaming toward the group of men. There was a flurry of confusion and gunfire in every direction. Billy looked down the barrel of Jasper's gun, but he fired faster and hit Jasper in the right arm. "Damn—missed." Billy said.

A bullet from Jasper's gun sung past Billy's head. Violet knocked a shot off on a man riding towards them; he fell off his horse with a loud crack—his neck broken. An arrow from one of the Apache warriors whizzed past Jasper's ear.

The Chief lined up one of Jasper's men in the sights of his Sharps Carbine. The man noticed and tried to retreat, but he was too late. After witnessing one of his partners being shot, the youngest of the group fled, unscathed. Jasper was alone, wounded and surrounded by Indians and the two compadres. He shot a furious glance at Billy and Violet and retreated. The war Chief let him go alive, as his bullet narrowly missed Jasper Smith's head.

The small battle was not without casualties on their side. A young Indian warrior lay on the blood-soaked grass. He was the same one who was angry at Billy and Violet's arrival. He was young, perhaps only eighteen or nineteen years old. Violet could see the pain and agony on his brave face, though he tried his best to hide it. He was bleeding to death from two bullet wounds in his left leg. The Chief rushed to his side. Violet then could see a younger version of the Chief in the young man who lay dying.

The Chief said, "Ciye... Hat'ugha?" He looked up to the sky as tears started to fill his war-hardened eyes. Violet rushed over to the Chief and his son. He turned to Violet. "Why has the Great Spirit done this to me? He is my only son." Violet took her bandanna off and wrapped it around the young man's leg above the bullet wound, as a tourniquet to help stop the bleeding.

"Hi-disho..." The young man angrily shoved Violet to the ground. She bounced right back up. She was just as stubborn as he was.

"Billy, I need your rag!" Billy cautiously gave Violet his bandanna. The Chief's son looked at Billy with suspicion.

He choked out, "I do not need help from this white man." She pressed down on the gunshot wounds to stop the bleeding. The young warrior suppressed a scream, as tears dripped down his temples. Violet's sharp eyes noticed a patch of yarrow not too far away from them.

"Pick some of that weed over there. It will help the Chief's son." Billy cooperated, but he took his time. She lifted the bloody rag. "I need your canteen."

He handed her his canteen, but drew away as if a snake was about to strike. She washed off the wound with the water, and rinsed out the rag. Violet crushed the yarrow leaves in her palms and then applied them to the wound, and then secured them with the rag. "It is not much, but it may help stop the bleeding." she said to the Chief.

The young warrior weakly spoke, as he grasped Violet's hand. "Ashoge... nah-lin." Any animosity that the chief's son held for Violet was wiped away. His face paled.

"Ah he ya he." Violet said reverently. His hand lost its grip on hers as he fainted. The Chief used a surprising amount of strength to pick up his son and placed him on his own horse. He rode away holding his son in his arms. The rest of the band followed after.

The acrid smoke of gunpowder still filled the air. Billy noticed the bodies of the three men lying on the ground. His stomach felt weak, he hadn't realized how horrible death was, even though it came to his enemies. His conscience wrestled with itself, whether or not to bury them. He didn't have a shovel, and there weren't enough rocks around to cover the bodies. His face turned hard and a chilling thought came to him, that they had come to kill them. They didn't deserve to be buried. Billy turned away from the terrible scene of death and began to put out the fire they had started just a moment before.

"So much for the beans..." he said to no one as he rinsed it off the tin plate and pan in the clear creek. He gathered up his gear and put it back in his saddle bag.

A single Apache appeared from the yellow cloud of dust and gun smoke. Like a phantom warrior, he sat on his horse as if he were waiting for something.

"What do they want now?" Billy asked.

Violet spoke quietly, "I think we're supposed to go with him."

"What makes you think that?" he said.

"Just trust me." Violet said as she got onto her painted pony. Billy obliged and got onto his horse. The warrior gestured them to follow.

# Chapter IV

They followed the silent Apache warrior. Neither Billy nor Violet knew where they were going, although she had the clearest idea out of the two. They rode over the prairie toward some green rolling hills. Tied to a stake were the horses the Apache warriors had been riding only a few minutes earlier. The tops of the tipis seemed to pierce the sky above the horizon. They had been led to the Lipan Apache camp.

The silent warrior directed them to the largest tipi on the camp's far side. The Chief sat in the center of the tipi. He motioned for Billy and Violet to sit. Billy's large eyes soaked it all in. The buffalo hides that lined the floor were thick and soft to the touch.

Violet looked natural and at ease as she sat there in the tipi. This sparked curiosity in Billy's mind about the young woman's identity. Why did she know so much about the Apache?

"I am Chief Running Buffalo." he said, "I brought you here because I wanted to thank you for helping my son. He will recover quickly thanks to you." He pointed towards Violet and Billy. "And to apologize for his stubbornness... we do not often accept help from strangers."

"It was our pleasure to help you in return for what you did for us," Violet said, "We are both alive, thanks to you."

"It is good that we understand each other. Jasper Smith is haiga—very bad. You are not the only ones to dislike him. He attacked my village two nights ago. He terrorized the women and children. He tried to shame and kidnap my daughter, but we fought back. Our medicine man was trampled by Jasper's horse, when he tried to stop them. My only regret is leaving Smith alive. He is like a cancer to both our peoples." He paused for a moment. "My son wishes to speak to you." He looked directly at Violet and motioned to the tipi directly across the way. Billy was about to get up but Running Buffalo gestured to him to stay sitting. She left, and Billy was left alone with the Chief.

Violet lifted the tanned buffalo hide that served as the door, inside lay the Chief's son. He tried to sit up as she entered, but winced.

"Thank you for helping me. I will be better sooner because of you." he said, and smiled weakly.

"It was my duty to help." she said.

He looked surprised. "I never thought that it would be a white woman's duty to help an Apache."

She tried to suppress a smile. "I am not just a white woman..." The Chief's son looked even more perplexed. "My father is an Indian." she said.

"Then we are the same. Both of our fathers are Indian." he said, "My name is White Horse."

"I am Violet."

He grabbed her hand as she stood up to leave. "Will I see you again?"

Violet blushed involuntarily. "Perhaps the Great Spirit will chance us to meet again." she said. White Horse smiled contentedly and then closed his eyes. Violet stepped outside and Billy was standing there with his arms crossed.

"What happened in there?" he said.

"Oh, he just wanted to thank me. How did it go with Running Buffalo?" she said coolly as she readied her horse.

"He told me that his scouting party will be watching for Jasper if he comes back."

"Sounds good to me, let's get a move on then."

As they rode away from the Apache camp she wondered if she would ever see White Horse again, or if he would just become a faded memory in time. They set out west into the sunset.

# Chapter V

For two days they rode. They only stopped to water their horses and to make camp in the evening. During their journey Violet noticed a far-off Apache scout every now and then, riding on the crest of a hill silhouetted by the sun. She never alerted Billy of this, but it seems they had made some friends and Running Buffalo made sure to have a scout watching over them.

They were starting to see the signs of civilization again, fence posts, cattle, and cow-pies.

"The next town is called Posthole." Billy said as he studied a roughed-up map of Texas.

"Sounds promising..." Violet said. Her sarcasm was evident. Both of the riders were parched from the dusty trail. They rode up to the saloon in the dusty, ragged looking town. They hitched their horses in front and walked inside. Billy turned to Violet jokingly.

"Now." Billy said, "You're not going to have any trouble in here, are you?"

Violet shot him a look that shut him up. They looked like a sight, both covered in trail dust from head-to-toe. Billy sat down at the large bar and Violet followed suit.

"I'll have a shot of whiskey, and a sarsaparilla for my friend." Billy whispered to Violet, "I remember that's your preferred choice." She wasn't sure if she should smile or hit him.

"Don't *you* cause any trouble now," she said. She winked and then took a swig from the brown glass bottle.

The barkeep was wiping down the counter and paused to look at Violet first and then his eyes rested on Billy. "You know," the barkeep said, "I swear I've seen you somewhere."

Billy looked surprised. "Really? I've never been around these parts."

The barkeep persisted, "I know I've seen you somewhere."

Violet's heart jumped up into her throat.

"I swear I've seen your face somewhere." he continued, "Maybe at the post office?" the barkeep tried to work out the mystery in his mind.

"Thanks for the drinks." she said as she put a fifty-cent piece on the counter, she turned to Billy. "Let's go."

He downed his shot of whiskey and followed her out. "Why so soon? Bye-golly, you sure are in a hurry ain'tcha?"

Violet turned to him as they were outside the saloon. "I don't like nosy strangers. We need to check out the post office."

They rode their horses down the dirty street to discover a small building with a wooden sign that read, Post and Federal Marshal's Office.

"I'm going to take a look-see." she said. Inside the window the chair at the Marshal's desk was empty. On the outer wall of the office were the wanted and missing posters. To her astonishment she saw a poster that caught her eye in large text:

WANTED!
Billy Colton and an Unknown Female
Accomplice for
MURDER
Reward $500

On the top was a photograph of Billy. Violet was in shock, but her pride was slightly wounded because she was only listed as 'an unknown female accomplice'.

"Take a look at this…" she said in a whisper.

"What is it?" Billy inquired as he got off his horse, his tone changed as he read the sign. "What the hell is this? This has to be Jasper Smith's doing… He's slyer than a fox with a key to the chicken coop."

"We're going to have to lay low." Violet cautioned.

"You're right. Everybody thinks I'm an outlaw." Billy said as his face turned white. He ripped the poster off the wall and stuffed it into his pocket. "I don't want people seeing my family name up there."

Violet felt pity and guilt for the helpful cowboy. "If we keep running people are going to suspect something." she said, "We need to rest and get more supplies. Hopefully no one else in town recognizes you."

Violet walked into the general store, Billy waited outside by the horses. As Violet was shopping Billy was even more conscious of his surroundings. He saw a rather stocky man walking toward the Marshal's office. The bright sun glinted off his polished metal badge. Billy turned his head and lowered his hat, in an attempt to obscure his face. The Marshal walked inside his office without noticing that the newest wanted poster was missing. Billy breathed a sigh of relief.

He could see from the large window that Violet was buying some foodstuffs and the saleswoman began showing her the dresses and other clothes. She picked out a frilly, modest blue gingham dress that was trimmed with crocheted white lace, some grey wool pants, a matching suit-jacket, a black bowler hat and a white shirt. She thanked the saleswoman, and paid for the goods.

She came out smiling with the packages wrapped in brown paper and string. "I got something for you." Violet said cheerfully as she handed him a package with the hat resting on top.

Billy was incredulous. "You really expect me to wear that?"

"Yes, I do. Plus I want you to get cleaned up." She pointed to the barber shop that stated 25 cents a bath, and 50 cents a shave. He left grumbling, "Since when do you tell me what to do?"

Violet asked him to meet her at the livery stable. Violet got herself cleaned and pretty and changed into her fancy little dress. A half hour later, Billy came out wearing the grey suit with his hair slicked back and his face clean-shaven.

"I guessed on the size." The jacket puckered a little at the shoulders. Violet tried to hold back a laugh as Billy looked out of his element. "You forgot something." Violet held up a black string tie.

"I don't think I know how to get this confounded thing on." he said in exasperation. Violet helped him get it tied. "I never thought I'd be wearing one of these things. I look like a dandy."

As she stepped back, Billy noticed how pretty she was. Her hour glass shape was accentuated by the feminine cut of the dress.

"You look convincing enough. You're just going to have to stow that old hat for a while." she said looking upward at him still wearing his worn-out, wide-brimmed brown hat.

Billy frowned as he put on the bowler. She crossed her arms and smiled, everything was going according to plan. They made their way to the hotel after the horses had been boarded.

Violet whispered to Billy, "Just follow my lead." As they entered, the desk clerk greeted them. "We would like one room please." Violet said with a sweet smile. Billy was surprised, to say the least. He tried to hide his expression by staring at his boots.

"Your names?" The hotel clerk asked dryly.

"Mr. and Mrs. Patterson. We were married last week." Violet looked at Billy and excitedly grabbed his hand. The desk clerk's eyebrow's rested over his tired, expressionless eyes. He scribbled the names down and handed them the key. "It's room 204, nice and comfy."

"Thank you sir." She flashed a bright smile.

They both went up to their room, Billy still very confused. After Violet locked the door he spoke up, "We're supposed to be married?"

"You're Rupert Patterson and I'm Maria. I figured we would be less suspicious if we were a well-to-do newlywed couple on their honeymoon.

Plus you needed to get the trail-dust off of you anyway."

Billy slumped into the chair, and tossed the bowler hat on the floor. His mind was exhausted. They both looked at the large bed. After a moment of silence passed between them, Billy figured it indecent to sleep in the same bed with Violet, and did the gentlemanly thing.

"You can have it ma'am." he said, "I'll sleep on the floor."

"Alright." Violet had to agree to the situation, she wanted to avoid anything that would make Billy even more uncomfortable. She shut the drapes and blew out the oil lamp. She received the best night's sleep that she had had in weeks, possibly months.

Billy was not so fortunate, while he laid on his bedroll on the hard-wood floor he could think of nothing but being perceived as an outlaw. He knew that neither he nor Violet murdered anyone, but fired in self-defense during an ambush, in fact the Indians did most of the killing. The very word 'outlaw' was something that he hated, it was associated with all sorts of bad men doing bad things. He didn't want to be lumped together with that kind of group. He was ashamed and angered that his family might see the posters, and think the worst of him. That was the last thing that he wanted. His body seethed with anger over Jasper Smith. He never thought he could hate someone so much in his life. As thoughts raced through his mind, a seed of doubt grew about the wisdom of his endeavor, but it was shoved away when he thought of Violet. He wanted nothing but to protect her.

The morning came sooner than he had expected and the peachy sunlight shone through the curtains and over Violet's face. She was still asleep. He studied her face in its most peaceful state. He reached out his hand. He was tempted to touch her cheek, but suddenly withdrew, knowing the consequences if she woke up. He wondered about this lady that he had known for such a short time but had turned his world upside-down. Who was she really? He had only known her for a few days, but it felt much longer than that. He felt a deep connection to her, but didn't really know her. He didn't even know why she wanted to go to San Angelo. She was a mystery to him. He sat back in the chair, waiting for her to awaken. Normally she was the first one to rise with the sun. He pondered the strange and dangerous turn his life had taken. He noticed his hands were shaking as Violet awoke.

"Good morning." he said.

She replied groggily, "We need to get a move on." She recalled the need to be polite, "How was your sleep?" she asked.

"Slept like a baby." he lied. "How 'bout yerself?"

"Just fine, I've slept too long. We need to get moving."

She was starting to display a pattern, Billy thought as he smiled a little.

They went down to the lobby to check out of their room. "Leaving so soon?" The desk clerk inquired.

"Yes, we have a lot of traveling to do." Violet said, smiling.

"Where are y'all headed?" For the first time Violet was speechless.

"Lubbock," Billy spoke up, "We're visiting family in Lubbock."

The desk clerk was displaying uncharacteristic curiosity. Violet's throat tightened as another one of her bad feelings came upon her.

She handed him the key, "Thank you very much sir."

Billy and Violet left the hotel together. "I think he suspects something. He was asking too many questions, especially since he seemed so disinterested last evening. Maybe he recognized you." she said, her brow furrowed.

"I doubt that, he was just being friendly." Billy dismissed the notion.

"Just because you took the poster down doesn't mean he hadn't seen it before. I'll pick up our things at the general store and we'll get out of here."

"You really don't trust anyone, do you? He was just making conversation."

"You're an outlaw now. You're going to have to start acting like one." Those words stung like venom in Billy's ears, his face turned red with anger. He never set out to become an outlaw.

Their horses were safe and sound at the livery stable. Violet had had a paranoid feeling that they might have been stolen during the night.

She had to get used to riding side-saddle like a proper lady. It was incredibly uncomfortable, and she didn't understand why anyone would have to do that, lady or not. As they passed the post office, Violet noticed that the hotel clerk moving his hands in an animated fashion as he spoke to the Marshal.

"We need to be careful." she said as they continued out of town, slowly. Just a few minutes later they heard the click clack of hooves behind them. They were being followed.

# Chapter VI

The Marshal approached them. "Howdy."

"Howdy." Billy replied.

"What brought you to Posthole?"

"Just passin' through."

"Heard you're on your way to Lubbock. You'll be going through Indian country, can't be too careful when traveling with the woman-folk." The Marshal said as he glanced at Violet.

She had to resist the urge to roll her eyes.

"Much obliged. We'll be careful." Billy said.

"Wouldn't want to hear of anything... distressing. Take care now."

He tipped his hat and left on his horse back to the post office. When they were a safe distance away Billy spoke again, "That was a close one. Your plan worked mighty well."

"Thank you." Violet smiled.

Billy couldn't help but wonder what began Violet's journey to San Angelo, and why she was so knowledgeable of the ways of the Indians. The curiosity had been eating away at his insides. He had to know soon. The conversation of the day was mostly uneventful and sparse. Once they made camp, Billy was going to ask once and for all. He had risked his life for her, not only that, he was now a fugitive of the law. The least she owed him was an answer to why they were going all the way to San Angelo, and who she was, really.

Dusk fell. They stopped to make camp. Soon a fire was blazing.

Billy decided to ask the question, "Who are you?"

"What do you mean?" Violet countered.

"You know what I mean," he said, "I hardly know anything about you. All I know is that you're from Missouri and you're headed for San Angelo. Normally, I wouldn't give a hoot, but we're gonna be spending a whole heck of a lot of time together."

Violet remembered the meeting with the Apache, and that must have set off Billy's suspicion. As much as she wished her true identity to be hidden among the right people, she owed him. Would he think any different of her if he knew the truth? She had to tell him. Eventually he would find out, and he might as well hear it from her.

"I am half Cherokee. It is something I have had to hide my entire life. People look at me different when they know who I really am, like something not quite human. I am lucky enough that I can pass for being white amongst the whites, but Indians recognize me as Indian."

Billy's face showed that he was surprised, but he half expected this outcome.

She waited for him to look at her differently, to judge her, but the expression in his eyes stayed the same. So she continued, "My father was going to become a medicine man, back in Georgia, long before the war. But as more lines were drawn between whites and Indians he became a horse-trader. He wanted to survive within the white man's world, he was given no choice. That was before they forced him out of his home and made him and the rest of the Tsalagi—our people—on the march to Indian Territory in the dead of winter. His mother—my grandmother—died on that trail, along with his sisters. My grandfather was shot by soldiers before they even left. Being the only one in his family left, he settled in Missouri. The mountains reminded him of his real home." She paused for a moment and pulled out a pendant on a long leather cord. "He gave me this to remind me. It's a symbol of medicine. It's supposed to grant protection." Billy stared at the pendant that she was clutching. Its beaded form was shaped like a wheel, and had many different colors. She quickly tucked it back under her blouse.

Billy stared at her, waiting for another explanation. "Is that how you know so much about the Indians—about the Apache?"

"Yes. I learned a lot from my father, he traded with many nations, including the Kiowa Apache. That's how I know some of their language."

"All my father ever did was own a ranch..." Billy was amazed by what he was hearing. This was the most that he had ever heard her say at one time. "What about your mother?" he inquired.

"My mother was an immigrant. She came from Germany as a young girl. Later she fell in love with my father. She was poor and he was as good a match as any. She knew that he would provide a good life for her. So they were married."

Billy thought he could get manage to ask her the question that was most weighing on his mind. "What's in San Angelo?"

Violet's face grew dark. He was worried she wouldn't answer him. In fact she didn't want to answer him. That was too much for him to know. She owed him.

"I think I've told you enough for one evening."

"I think it would be good for me to know, since I am going with you all this way."

"You didn't have to stay with me."

Billy was a quiet for a moment. "I wanted to."

Violet indignantly questioned his motives, "Why do you want to go with me to San Angelo—adventure?"

Billy felt belittled, "Well I'm kind of stuck with you now. Ain't I? I'm an outlaw because of you. It's not like I can just go back home. Jasper and his gang want to throw me a neck-tie party. I've sacrificed a lot for you, but it wasn't an accident."

Violet's eyes widened. She finally realized why Billy had stuck with her. He was falling in love with her.

This complicated matters. She didn't want to become attached to Billy. She had made a promise. She also didn't want to tell him the reason because it would break his heart. It might drive him away. But where would he go? She put him in this situation. He had saved her life. He was considered an outlaw for protecting her. He was on the run because of *her*.

"Goodnight, Billy."

She pulled her blanket up to her face, tears forming in her eyes, and tried to sleep. She tried to forget what he had said, and what she had felt.

# Chapter VII

Billy woke before dawn. There were still a few red coals glowing in the white ashes of the dead fire. Violet was still asleep. He began to realize that it didn't matter to him why she was going to San Angelo. He wanted to go with her anyway. He would find out her reasons sooner or later, but it didn't really matter to him just now. It would be more rewarding for her to finally trust him, and tell him her motive on her own accord. Billy tried to get back to sleep but he failed, so he started to pack up camp.

\* \* \*

Jasper Smith walked into the post office of Posthole, Texas. He noticed the poster which he had so painstakingly sent out to the surrounding towns had been torn down. The thud of his boots in front of the desk awoke the good-natured Marshal.

"How can I help you sir? If you want the mail, it won't be coming for a good three hours."

Jasper spat his tobacco chaw carelessly on the floor. "My poster's missing. Did you happen to see a couple ride through town yesterday?" Even with his right arm bandaged and in a sling Jasper looked formidable.

The Marshal pushed back his hat while he recalled his memory of yesterday, "I believe I did. Nice couple—newlyweds, heading for Lubbock. What fer?"

Jasper gritted his teeth. "You're a fool. That was Billy Colton and some woman. They're wanted for the murder of my friends—highly respected gentlemen of great rapport." He slammed another poster down on the Marshal's desk.

Jasper stormed out of the post office. "Boys," he said, "it looks like they're ahead of us."

There were just two other men with him, but this time with more firepower and experience than the last group. One man had a bowler hat covering his shaggy mane of light red hair, with a shotgun slung over his shoulder. The other had a three-day beard, wild eyes, and he had a pistol situated on the left side of his hip. They all started their horses at full gallop out of Posthole.

* * *

On their second day Violet had given up riding side-saddle. They continued to wander the vast Texas prairie. The bright sun beat down brutally upon them as they led their horses.

By the third day out of Posthole she noticed the Apache scout was no longer shadowing them. "There goes our guardian angel." she said to herself.

"What was that?"

"Nothing."

Billy just accepted it as one of her peculiarities. Violet noticed a ragged wagon, seemingly abandoned.

"I'm going to check this out." She moved closer to inspect the scene. A sudden unnatural quiet filled the air, the birds stopped singing and everything became still. "Something's not right here." she said as she looked around.

A shot was fired from behind a large limestone boulder. Their horses whinnied.

"Get down!" Violet shouted. She and Billy hid behind the wagon out of the way of the gunfire.

"Who could that be?" he said to her, surprised.

"I don't think any of Jasper's cronies could have snuck ahead of us."

They heard a voice from behind the boulder.

"Hola amigos! Give us the horses and we let you go." The voice had a thick Mexican accent.

"Bandidos," Billy said angrily. Violet pulled out her pistol.

The voice continued. "There are many of us. You are outnumbered." Billy grabbed for the rifle hanging from his saddle. The voice continued, "Muchacho, give us your guns and horses and you and the señorita will go free."

"Like hell," Billy said as he pulled the lever on his Henry lever-action rifle and aimed for the boulder. "How do we know you're not bluffing, amigo?"

"Don't taunt him." Violet quietly cautioned.

They could here several pistols cocking.

"Dammit." Billy frowned, he had guessed wrong.

From below the wagon Violet could see the boots of a bandido slowly making his way towards them. The large, sun-shaped silver spurs glinted as he walked. The tops of sombreros popped up from behind the rocks and brush. Through the ripped canvas of the wagon Violet could see that the main bandido was wearing a large black sombrero ornamented with gold stitching on the band. He seemed to be their leader.

"Do not be afraid," he said, "we only want to take your horses and weapons."

His hands were up in the air in a gesture of peace. He spoke more eloquently than the voice behind the boulder.

Another one of the bandidos fired towards the wagon. "Hijo de Puta!" The main bandido spoke angrily in the direction of the man who fired the shot. Billy shot back, a flurry of gunfire ensued. In the confusion the main bandido managed to seize Violet. The gunfire stopped. The bandido had his pistol pointed at Billy. Billy had his rifle pointed towards him.

"On the other hand," the bandido said, "the Comanche might pay mucho for this bonita." He sniffed her hair and smiled greasily. Billy tried to control his anger as he aimed for the bandido's head. He didn't want to miss and accidently shoot Violet. She elbowed the bandido hard in the stomach causing him to buckle over. She whipped around and pointed her pistol at him. His eyes were wide with surprise. The bandido put his shaking hands up slowly.

The two gunmen and Jasper Smith watched from a hill as the Billy and Violet had a standoff with the bandidos.

"I don't want them to get to them before we do." the wild-eyed gunman said through gritted teeth.

The other gunman spoke in a lilting Irish accent. "Take it easy Lefty. We'll get to them alright. I'm going to give them a little warning."

Beneath the hill the loud boom of a shotgun was heard. Birds flew from their hiding places in the tall grass. It blew a large hole through the wagon cover, and went through a bandido in its path. Billy, Violet, and the bandidos all looked around for the origin of the shot.

"Who was that? Are they your friends?" The main bandido pointed his pistol at Violet, panicked. The rest of the bandidos aimed at the hill. A shotgun blast hit the main bandido in the side and threw him to the ground.

"What in tarnation?" Billy said, turning his head toward the hill. The other bandidos began to fire at the hill. Billy and Violet got on their horses in an attempt to escape.

"Great job O'Leary. Now we'll never get 'em." Lefty said angrily. He grabbed the shotgun from O'Leary and shot at Billy and Violet. The shot hit next to her horse and spewing gravel and dirt in the air. The horse toppled violently and threw Violet.

"What the hell are you doing? The next time you take my shotgun you'll be a dead man."

O'Leary repossessed his shotgun from Lefty. The gunmen were left trying to defend themselves from the shots fired from the bandidos beneath the hill.

Violet landed on a sharp limestone boulder, the brunt of the impact was taken by her ribcage and her left shoulder. She rolled to the ground, she felt a piercing pain in her side and she couldn't move her left arm. She clawed at the dirt and gravel trying to get up. Blood dripped down her fingernails. She looked at her horse lying on the ground beside her. Its front left leg was broken. Fear filled its large dark eyes. Billy removed the saddlebags from her horse and threw them over his shoulder.

Violet weakly spoke, "Get out of here Billy. They want to kill you."

"Stubborn woman…" he said as he picked Violet up and put her on his saddle. He cocked his rifle and put it against the suffering animal's skull. In an instant the gallant painted steed was dead. Tears of sadness, pain and anger dripped down Violet's face as she and Billy rode away from the quarreling bandidos and the mysterious shootists on the hill.

# Chapter VIII

"We need to get you to a doctor." Billy said. They had already distanced themselves several miles from the bandidos and the mysterious shootists on the hill. The sun began to set. Long shadows fell upon the prairie. He could tell that there was something wrong with her shoulder, and a few of her ribs had been broken.

He held her in his arms as she began to drift in and out of consciousness, her head bobbing up and down as they rode. His new shirt was stained with her blood.

"Hang in there Violet." he said to her, but she didn't answer. Her eyes were closed but she was still breathing. He pushed his steady quarter horse to its limit.

"I've got to save her." he said to no one. The next town and the next doctor were at least five miles away. After several more arduous minutes of riding the mare was wheezing and he knew that if he didn't stop pushing her they would be out a horse.

"Alright." He stopped riding, and took Violet's limp body off his saddle. He laid her gently on the ground next to an oak tree.

Her body was bruised and broken. Her left shoulder seemed unnaturally squared-off, and she was bleeding from the intrusion of gravel in her ribcage. He caught himself wishing that Violet were conscious to give him instruction. He had to improvise. He took off his jacket and his shirt. He ripped the fancy white shirt into thick strips and wrapped them around her rib cage to stop some of the bleeding.

The shoulder was going to be more difficult. He remembered that his little brother once dislocated his shoulder after falling out of a tree. Billy watched his pa set it. He tried to recollect the details of that day. The last thing he wanted to do was to hurt Violet even more. His hands shook as he grabbed ahold of her arm. He sent a rare prayer out to the heavens, "Oh God, please help me do this right."

He bent her elbow into a right angle and slowly began to move her bent arm to the left. There was a loud pop. Her shoulder appeared normal again. He then put the rest of his shirt onto her arm and tied it around her neck as a sling. He picked her up and carefully and placed her on his saddle, he tied her to the saddle so she wouldn't fall. He walked his horse carrying Violet to the town. He hoped that the mysterious shooters and bandidos were distracted enough by each other's gunfire to be far behind them.

It was pitch black by the time they made it into town. Billy kicked open the doctor's door holding Violet in his arms. He startled a small bespectacled man holding a candle.

"Are you the doctor?"

"Yes. What's the emergency?"

Billy placed Violet in the leather operating chair. "She was thrown from her horse."

The doctor inspected her. "It looks as though she has a few broken ribs..." He noticed her arm in the sling.

"She dislocated her shoulder." Billy informed the doctor.

"Did you reset it?"

He hesitated a moment before answering, "I did."

"Good work, young man. I'm going to clean the wounds." The doctor gingerly unwrapped the bandages that Billy had so carefully put around her ribcage. "You might want to step outside for a moment."

Billy left the doctor's office to ensure Violet's privacy. After a moment it was safe to step back inside. The strong odor of witch hazel hung in the air. The bodice of her dress had been cut away, her wounds cleaned and her chest wrapped with bandages. The doctor removed the sling made out of Billy's shirt and replaced it with a more civilized one made of thick canvas.

"When will she wake up, doc?"

"She has lost quite a bit of blood, but we can try to wake her." He selected smelling salts from a shelf with a large variety of bottles. "This might do the trick." He uncorked the small bottle and placed it directly under her nose. Violet's head shifted and her eyes opened. Her eyes squinted at Billy.

"Why aren't you wearing a shirt?" He had forgotten for a moment that he had turned his shirt into bandages. He ran outside to put another one on. Violet relapsed back into unconsciousness. The doctor tried a different bottle of salts and she was awake again, her head pounding.

"Where am I? Who are you?" Violet inquired as she tried to recollect the events that had led her there. She instinctively grabbed the pair of scissors from the tray table with her good arm and pointed them at the doctor. "Where's Billy?"

Billy came back inside with his old red shirt thrown over his shoulders.

"Who is this man?" she asked again, still pointing the small scissors at the doctor's neck. Billy stood there dumbfounded in silence, waiting for the doctor to respond.

"I'm Doctor Wilson."

She dropped the scissors on the tray table, causing the other instruments to clang and rattle.

"Why didn't you say that before?"

Violet closed her eyes once again, exhausted.

The doctor was shocked, "She must have been severely traumatized. You're going to need this," The doctor shakily handed Billy a bottle of Jim Beam whiskey. "It will help to dull the pain and relax her."

Billy knew that Violet would object. "Why don't you give it to her yourself?"

"Normally my patients don't threaten me."

Billy paid the doctor two silver dollars. He put Violet's good arm around his shoulder, and helped her out of the doctor's office. Violet's head was spinning and she could hardly breathe. She could barely remember what had happened since running into the bandidos. The ride to the town was a dark, disjointed, and painful blur.

"We need to find you somewhere where you can rest." Billy said.

The narrow street was lit only by lamplight. The little that Violet could see of the town grew darker, and darker, and she passed out. Billy picked her up and carried her limp body into the hotel lobby. The older woman at the desk was alarmed to see the wounded, unconscious woman.

"Is she alright?" The woman said.

"She was thrown from her horse. She's just seen the doctor."

"Well that's a start. We'll make sure you can both rest."

The woman had a stocky build and was surprisingly strong. She assisted Billy in getting Violet up the stairs.

"Bless her heart, poor little dear. It must have been a terrifying ordeal for her." The woman empathized. Billy carefully tucked Violet into bed.

"Well, if you need anything just call for Maggie. I'm the owner of this establishment."

"Thank you kindly," Billy said.

"Oh, I'm going to need your names for the book."

Billy recalled the names that Violet had used last, "Rupert and Maria Patterson."

"Poor little dear..." she said as she looked at the pathetic stranger in the bed and left the room.

It looked to Billy as if Violet was asleep. He placed his hand on her forehead, it was damp but she didn't have a fever. She was breathing shallowly, most likely due to her three broken ribs. He didn't want to leave her alone in the hotel room, but his horse was still hitched outside and it needed water. As he closed the door he prayed that she would be safe without him.

There was always the threat of Jasper and whomever shot at him and Violet looming over his head, not only that, but the very *law* wanted him for murder.

He took his horse over to the water trough next to the saloon. He stroked his tired horse as it drank eagerly. "You've done good."

He knew that Violet would have to get another horse or they would have to use some other mode of transportation. But did they have the money? He was running low on the money he had earned from helping with last year's cattle sale. He had no clue to the amount of money Violet had with her.

Billy ear's perked up when he heard the steady clip-clop of hoofbeats coming into town. On top of the lonely steed was a dark, bent figure obscured by the shadows of the lamplight.

# Chapter IX

The steed stopped at the steps of the saloon. The hunched rider tumbled to the ground. Billy rushed over to help. He recognized the black and gold sombrero.

"Socorro, have mercy señor." The bandido pleaded, as one hand clutched the oozing red wound on his stomach, and the other reached out to Billy. His eyes widened after he recognized the man standing over him as one of his attempted victims. "I will die." he said, resigned, and shut his eyes.

Billy wrestled with the idea of helping someone who had threatened to kidnap Violet and whose men tried to kill him. The very memory of that moment surrounded by bandidos churned up hatred inside of Billy. He turned around and walked away.

The dying bandido's plea for mercy haunted and disgusted him. If the bandido died alone in the street, Billy would be responsible. Perhaps he would show more mercy than the bandido would if he were in the same situation.

He walked back to the dying man, who was now unconscious. He took the bandido's gun and dragged him by the boots into the doctor's office.

"What now?" The doctor said irksomely, after recognizing Billy.

"He's been shot."

"You certainly seem to attract a lot of trouble." The doctor complained.

Billy sat in the chair as he watched the doctor work on the bandido. He watched, and waited patiently, his hat over one eye as the doctor removed each piece of shot.

"I need to speak with this gentleman alone." Billy said once the doctor pulled out the last metal ball.

"He's all yours." The doctor said as he left to go to the back room to dispose of the gauze and to wash the blood-stained implements.

"Why have you helped me?" The bandido asked, breathing arduously.

"Only one reason..." Billy said, "Who shot you?"

"Los pistoleros?"

"Sí, los pistoleros." he said as he stood up and walked toward the bandido, his boots making a slow cli-clunk, cli-clunk.

The bandido reached for his gun in his holster, but to his surprise he saw his pistol tucked in the front of Billy's gun belt.

"They killed my men and left me for dead. I do not know who they are." The bandido turned his head away from Billy. His face was covered in sweat.

"Did they say anything? What did they look like?" Billy searched for some clue to the identity of the men who fired the shots from the hill.

"They did not rob me or my men. They said they did not want any witnesses… They thought I was dead, but I have lived."

"What else did they say? I know you have more to tell."

"They said they were looking for a man… a man and a señorita." The bandido paused thoughtfully for a moment, "Could it be you señor?"

"Don't ask any more questions or I'll tell the doctor to take those bandages right off and have him put the shot right back in."

"You wouldn't do that, señor." Billy gave him a look as if to challenge that. "They were led by a tall, grande man, his arm was bandaged. There were two others with him. One was joven and loco. The one that carried a shotgun did not sound like a Texian."

"That's good enough."

The doctor walked back into the room.

"Thanks for your services doc." Billy tossed two silver dollars to the doctor, which were caught between his palms.

The door slammed shut behind Billy as he walked away, still in possession of the bandido's pistol.

He led his horse to the livery stable. A boy of about twelve holding a lantern greeted Billy.

"Take care of her now. She's had a rough ride." Billy instructed the boy as he handed him the reins.

"Yes sir."

"Do you have any horses for sale?"

"No sir. We won't have any head until tomorrow morning when Mr. McCarthy comes in with a fresh herd."

"Much obliged..." Billy paused for a second. "What town is this?"

"Deer Creek, sir."

"Thanks kid."

Billy flipped a coin to the boy, which was eagerly caught. Billy went back to the hotel to check on Violet. He opened the door and saw Violet on the bed. She was breathing in short, labored breaths, but she was still breathing. She jerked awake when he shut the door.

"What happened?" She put her good hand on her head to stop the throbbing.

"You were thrown from your horse. I took you to the doctor."

Violet recalled pointing the scissors at the bespectacled man. She groaned.

"He told me to give you this." He held up the bottle of Jim Beam whiskey.

Violet's vision was foggy and she couldn't decipher the words on the bottle.

"What is it?"

Billy paused for a moment and looked at the bottle, and responded, "Medicine."

He put the bottle up to her mouth, and she took a swig. She spewed the liquid out. "This is whiskey! I don't need the white man's firewater!"

"Fine then," Billy took the bottle and gave himself a swig. "I do." Billy plunked himself down on the chair next to the bed.

Violet had never felt so much pain in her life. She had been thrown from a horse before when she worked with her father, it was inevitable working with horses, but this was by far her worst accident. She could barely remember the events from that day, and she began to fall into a groggy, delirious sleep.

Her dreams were vivid and colorful. She could see her horse, from the first time she spotted him in a herd of wild mustangs. She and her father roped him, she broke and trained him. She never named him—he didn't need a name because he was as wild and free as the prairie wind. She dreamt of the moments of riding him from her home, across Indian Territory and all the way to Texas. It was a solitary journey and her horse was her only traveling companion. Then there was the painful memory—the flash of the broken leg, the eyes full of fear, and the gunshot. Then her horse was gone.

Violet woke up in a cold sweat. She was breathing rapidly. The sound of the gunshot seemed to reverberate like the ringing in her ears. She could feel the tears well up in her eyes. She didn't cry often, but she couldn't control her emotions any longer, her grief was too great.

It was morning. She looked at the chair, it was empty—Billy wasn't there. She was wearing her old patterned shirt over her bandages. The hotel owner knocked on the door. Violet quickly wiped away the tears with her sleeves. Strong and savory breakfast smells wafted through the air. Maggie was carrying a tray. "I brought you breakfast. Your husband requested it for you."

"Husband?" Violet questioned confusedly.

"Oh dear, you must've been thrown good to forget a man like that."

"Oh, you mean..." She stopped herself from saying Billy's name and recalled their aliases. "Rupert. We've only been married for a week."

Violet thanked Maggie for the vittles and mustered up a smile. There was a bowl of grits, fried eggs, bacon, and a cup of coffee. Violet hadn't eaten anything since yesterday morning, she was certainly hungry but her appetite had fled.

* * *

Billy watched the pink sunrise over the stretches of dew-laden grass. He waited for the man with the fresh herd of horses to come into town. He knew that in order for both him and Violet to survive she would have to have a horse to escape whoever was after them. A single rider appeared on the horizon, but there were no other horses.

Billy turned to the boy at the livery. "You did say Mr. McCarthy would come with a fresh heard this morning?"

"Yes sir."

"Is that him?" Billy pointed to the lone rider on the horizon.

The boy squinted to see. "No sir. Looks like one of his hired hands."

Billy rested his elbows on the livery's corral fence waiting for the rider to meet them. By further inspection Billy could tell the rider was just a simple cowboy, and he looked exhausted.

"Where's Mr. McCarthy?" Billy demanded.

"He's not here. The horses were scattered and taken by Indians. I don't know where he's at." The cowboy was breathing heavily out of fear and exhaustion from the chase. Billy turned to the boy. "Do you have any more horses coming in?"

"Not for a while, mister…"

Billy turned to the cowboy. "Much obliged."

He walked away and angrily kicked the dust in the street when he was out of sight. This meant that they were going to be stuck here for a while. He felt that he had failed Violet in some way by not procuring her a horse. His shoulders grew heavy with the thought of whoever must be chasing them. He recalled the bandido's description from the night before. There were three men. One with a bandaged arm, one with a foreign accent carrying a shotgun, the other was young and crazy, and carried a pistol. He didn't have the heart to face Violet and tell her that he didn't find a horse for her. At least she was safe in the hotel under the care of Maggie.

Billy had a hangover, and he needed something to cure his ails from drinking about half a bottle of Jim Beam the night before. He walked into the saloon. He situated himself on one of the barstools facing the mirror so he could see if anyone came through the swinging doors. He was beginning to think like an outlaw. It was still early in the morning and the bar was quiet.

"Got anything to cure a hangover?" Billy asked.

"Sure do." The old bartender with white whiskers poured some tomato juice, added a few generous dashes of hot red pepper Tabasco sauce, and cracked a whole egg into the tall glass.

"Drink up. It's good for you." The bartender smiled eagerly, his voluminous handlebar mustache seemed to rise with his grin.

Billy seemed a little skeptical, but gave a look of 'here-goes-nothing' and chugged the red liquid. He scowled as he swallowed. "Not bad."

In the reflection of the back bar mirror Billy noticed a lone man sitting in the corner. Turning around he recognized the distinctive sombrero. It was the bandido. He hadn't thought of where he might have gone after the doctor's visit. He walked over to the bandido's table.

"What are you doing here?" Billy said.

"Just having a drink, señor."

"Why don't you ride on outta here?"

"I have no weapon, no way to defend myself, and three men already think I'm muerto. Now can you understand, señor?"

"Yes, I can understand. Only a yellow-belly like you who tries to kidnap innocent women would hide in a hole like a cockroach."

The bandido clenched his jaw. "I am no cucaracha!" He slammed his glass on the table. "You took my weapon señor."

Billy was coolheaded, "Only to defend myself."

The bandido paused. "I did not tell you everything last night."

"What didn't you tell me?" Billy tried to stare the truth out of the bandido.

"Los pistoleros, they know where you are. They are coming to town today. If you give me my weapon back, I will help you."

"How do I know I can trust you now?"

"They killed all of my men, and left us to die like dogs in the sun. If you will give me back my weapon I do not care why they want to kill you. I only want revenge. It is not you I want to kill." He looked Billy over and looked back at his glass. "When the gunmen ride into town today, will you believe me?"

Billy thought for a moment. "Yes, but only then." He walked away leaving the bandido angry and defenseless.

# Chapter X

Jasper and the gunmen waited outside of the sleepy little town of Deer Creek as the sun began to rise.

"So how are we gonna get 'em?" Lefty spoke anxiously while holding a plate of beans.

"We'll wait." Jasper said.

"When the sun is up they'll be easier to hit… if necessary." O'Leary spoke in his quiet voice as if he had some authority—he at least had the experience, shown by the notches carved into the stock of his double-barreled ten gauge shotgun, representing each person captured or killed.

Lefty was growing impatient. He wrung his hands as O'Leary lit up a cigar, and leaned back on his elbows. Lefty wanted to prove his competency as a bad man. He was green, and he didn't want anyone to know it.

"We'll wait until they don't expect us to come… to make them think we didn't follow them. We'll surround the hotel." Jasper said and then spat on the ground.

"Jasper is right." O'Leary agreed, "There really is no rush, the girl is wounded and the boy won't leave until she's better. Sounds like a plan."

"Eat your beans, Lefty." Jasper growled.

Lefty was fed-up from the disrespect of his comrades. He was left impatient for the moment of the kill.

* * *

Violet finally worked up enough of an appetite to start on the coffee and grits. Billy came back into the room. He had a tired and worried look on his face.

"How ya doing?" he said. He flipped a chair around, pulled it to her bedside and sat down. "That breakfast sure looks tasty." He flashed one of his brilliant smiles.

"I forgot how long it's been since I've eaten anything." she said as she moved her spoon around the bowl of grits.

Billy was silent for a moment as he watched Violet. She could sense something was eating at Billy, but she couldn't decide what.

Billy decided to spit it out and tell her, "I couldn't get you a horse. The livery was supposed to have more in today, but..." he didn't want to mention how bad the situation was, "it'll be a long while before they'll get anymore."

"We'll just have to improvise..." Violet tried to hide her disappointment with positivity.

"I guess so." he said.

He worried about Violet—about her injuries. He didn't know how long it was going to take for her to be fully healed. He had never seen her so physically weak. It tugged at his heart to see an otherwise strong woman so vulnerable.

He pondered the bandido's words. What might happen if the gunmen did know that he and Violet had made it to the town and were in the hotel? He didn't want to tell Violet about the bandido, afraid that it would distress her further.

"Are you feeling any better?" Billy repeated his concern.

She took a deep breath in and felt a sharp pain like hundreds of tiny needles in her chest. "I'm fine." She tried to cover up the lie with a smile, but it was weak.

"Let me know if you need anything, I'm going downstairs to rustle up some vittles fer myself."

Billy walked downstairs and into the dining room of the hotel. He sat down at one of the many empty round tables and set his hat down on the chair beside him. It was still too early in the morning for any other patrons. Maggie was standing near the counter.

"Do you have any more of those eggs and grits?" he said.

"Oh, I believe I do."

She rushed back into the kitchen and brought him the same breakfast of grits, bacon, eggs and coffee. He thanked her and eagerly ate. Billy needed information about how he and Violet would eventually get out of town, if the supply of horses to the livery had been delayed indefinitely.

"Say, do you happen to know when the next stage comes into town?" he said.

"That won't be until next week on Monday morning." Maggie replied.

Being that it was Friday, it would be three more days until the coach arrived.

"Do you know where it'll be headed?"

"The line starts in Austin and goes all the way out west to Fort Concho, just north of San Angelo."

Perfect, he thought.

"Much obliged, Maggie." he said as he raised the mug of coffee to his lips. Once he finished his breakfast he said, "We'll be staying here for a few days at least 'til the stagecoach comes into town."

Maggie nodded. Billy began to walk back upstairs to check on Violet, he had never been worried about someone so much in his life.

A bullet whizzed past his ear causing him to jump for his pistol. The hotel lobby window had a hole in it the size of a dime. He looked through the window but there was no sign of a shootist. He took out his pistol and walked onto the hotel porch cautiously. Still, the streets were empty. Where had that bullet come from? Could it the same Pistoleros the bandido spoke of?

The street was eerily quiet and he searched for a sign of the gunmen. He heard the creaking of the saloon doors. He quickly turned to the left. There was the worthless bandido, he whispered, "Give me my gun, señor."

Billy looked down he had forgotten he had left the bandido's pistol tucked in the front of his gun belt.

"Why should I trust you?"

"Please, I will help you. The Pistoleros want to kill you, señor."

Billy didn't have time to think. He grabbed the gun and tossed it to the bandido, hoping that he was telling the truth.

"I will help you señor." The bandido said as he looked him in the eye. There was truth there.

The street was still quiet, but Billy could see the shadow of the shootist behind the livery stable, so he took aim.

* * *

Violet heard the first gunshot. Her pistol and gun belt was hanging on the back of the chair just out of reach. She stretched her arm out to get it, but a sharp pain in her ribs stopped her. Her heart pumped faster. She felt fingertips brush against the hard leather. She couldn't get a grip on the holster. She stretched her arm further and managed to touch it, but instead of grasping it, it was knocked to the floor. She had to get up, but she was weak and had scarce moved since the other night. She had to get her weapon to defend herself—she wouldn't die in her bed.

She heard a door creak open. She had the terrifying feeling that someone else was in the hotel, someone dangerous, and she couldn't reach her gun. She tried with greater fervor to get out of bed to it. She managed to sit up with incredible pain, using her good right arm for support. She heard the sounds of boots on hardwood, *thump, thump, thump,* as they ran down the upstairs hallway towards her room. Beads of sweat formed on her forehead as she rolled out of her bed and landed on her knees, she then tried to grasp her gun belt with her right hand, her left arm restrained in a sling.

The door swung open and her head tilted up, there stood a man she had never seen before. He had a pistol sitting on the left side of his hip. He grabbed her with both arms around the waist, with her pistol just out of reach. She kicked, flailed, and punched at him with her good arm but she was too weak. He twisted her good arm and pinned it against her back. He threw her down to the ground, she cried as he slammed a knee into her back to keep her down. She yelled for help but it was muffled as he put a hand over her mouth— she could taste the mud and sweat. He took his bandanna and tied it over her mouth as a gag. She was dragged from the hotel room and through the long upstairs hallway, and down the back outside stairway.

\* \* \*

Billy heard the muffled scream. He ran into the hotel lobby and up the stairs. He checked their room—there was no sign of Violet. He stumbled over her gun belt as he walked out the door. He knew something was terribly wrong if Violet did not have her pistol. He picked it up and stuck it in his trousers—he might need an extra gun. He searched the hallway and frantically realized Violet wasn't in the hotel. He busted out the front doors and into the street. His ears perked up as he heard a pistol cock. A man to his right was holding Violet captive and had his pistol pointed at her temple. Billy could see something out of the corner of his eye, it was another gunman, and

Billy was soon staring down the twin barrels of a shotgun. He saw Jasper Smith ten feet away on his horse. Billy's jaw clenched and his fists shook in anger.

"We've come to get ye Billy," the friendly, lilting Irish accent of the man holding the shotgun to his face seemed out of place, "ye can come with us to Mustang Ridge where ye will face a fair trial for yer crimes, or this can get difficult so we have to shoot ye. Yer choice."

Billy's eyes darted around, looking for any method of attack or escape. The bandido was nowhere in sight. That yellow-bellied coward, he thought to himself. Billy was already outmanned, and if he tried to draw his pistol, the man holding Violet captive might kill her, or the already poised gunman with the shotgun might shoot him. It was too much of a risk.

A single shot rang out in the air; the horse of O'Leary jumped and ran in circles, spooked. The bandido walked through the saloon doors as he downed a shot of whiskey and threw the glass on the floor, it shattered while he cocked his pistol to get ready for the next shot. The bandido had kept his word.

Lefty held on to Violet, but began to back off into an alleyway behind the hotel for cover, Billy followed after Lefty. Jasper fired at the bandido, but missed. O'Leary struggled to regain control of his horse, but once he did he aimed at the bandido, the shotgun blast splintered the saloon door.

"Forget about the bandido, O'Leary! It's Colton we want." Jasper said. He grabbed ahold of his Texas tie lasso and started to swing. Lefty dragged Violet through the alleyway, her boot heels making two even tracks in the dirt. Billy ran after him. Jasper swung his lasso and aimed for Billy's neck, but it settled around his waist. Jasper pulled his horse back and Billy was flung backwards. His horse dragged him through the alleyway, followed by a trail of dust. Lefty stood still pointing the pistol at Violet's head. Both Lefty and O'Leary were confused—this was not how they had planned it.

The bandido fired his last bullet at O'Leary and missed. Jasper continued to ride. The big black horse dragged its human cargo to the outskirts of the small town. O'Leary sheathed his shotgun and followed Jasper reluctantly. Lefty threw the exhausted Violet onto his saddle, and followed after Jasper.

"Don't try anything now, I ain't afeard to shoot a lady." Lefty said. Violet could feel the cold muzzle of the gun pressing into her back.

# Chapter XI

Jasper dragged Billy through the dirt of the empty main street, and out of town. Billy struggled to untie himself as he was being dragged. It was useless. The horse was galloping as if its master were the devil. The rope was so tight that Billy's fingers couldn't even slide between it and his chest. If only he had his Bowie knife, one cut and he would be free. The lariat continued to tighten as he was pulled faster, and it slid up to Billy's armpits. He coughed as the loose dirt and dust flew into his mouth. Jasper seemed to ride over the roughest parts of gravel and rocks to torture Billy as much as possible.

Violet watched from Lefty's horse with a gun to her back as Billy was brutally dragged behind Jasper's horse. They rode to a lone, old, large sycamore tree. She observed in horror that the branches were high enough and big enough to hang a man.

Billy was weak and beat, spread out flat on his stomach. Jasper got down from his horse and slowly walked toward Billy. Billy reached for his gun, which had managed to stay in the holster, but Jasper was too quick and took it before his weakened victim could. Jasper smiled like a triumphant, teasing child as he held up the pistol just out of Billy's reach. He then tossed it aside next to the base of the old tree.

"Let's have a good ol' fashioned lynching!" Jasper yelled. O'Leary's eyebrows lowered over his grey eyes, he had not expected this outcome. The understanding was, when he took the job that the fugitive would be brought back to Mustang Ridge to face a trial. Although O'Leary was a bounty hunter, he disliked killing a man unless there was no other available course of action. He hadn't expected a lynching. That would hurt his good reputation of bringing men back to the law. He already disliked the fact that Lefty kidnapped Violet as leverage, but that was Lefty's choice, O'Leary had had no part of that decision.

Jasper untied the rope from his saddle horn, and plucked a rock the size of his enormous fist from the ground. He tied it to the end of the rope and threw it over one large protruding branch.

Lefty twisted Violet's wrist with a vice-like grip to keep her from resisting. The gun was plunged deeper into her back. She felt totally helpless, and she was enraged.

"Jasper," O'Leary pleaded, "perhaps we should reconsider. Wouldn't it be finer justice to have him hang in Mustang Ridge?"

Jasper shot an angry glance at O'Leary. "Justice? Who said anything about justice?" He laughed.

"I don't deal in matters of revenge, Mr. Smith. If that's what you want, I will have no part of it." O'Leary said coolly as he looked Jasper in the eye.

"Well, you're fired. And don't expect any of the reward money."

"I don't." O'Leary rode away on his horse. His grey eyes expressed sadness tinged with guilt as he looked back at Violet and Billy.

Jasper started to walk back toward his victim again. Billy remembered something that he hoped Jasper had forgotten—he still had Violet's gun. He tipped himself over onto his left shoulder as to conceal the weapon that was still in his trouser pant. He took the pistol with his right arm and waited for Jasper to come closer. He could see Jasper's legs, and that was about it. He took the shot. Jasper jumped back in a frenzied panic, and began to hop around on his left foot. The bullet was lodged in his right foot. His black leather boot became soaked in blood. He lost his balance and fell to the ground.

He screamed, "You shot me! That damn son of a bitch shot me!"

"What do you want me to do Jasper?" Lefty said.

"Shoot him!" Jasper screamed.

Lefty removed the pistol from Violet's back, and pointed it at Billy. With a sudden rush of adrenaline she kicked back at Lefty knocking the gun out his hand before he could fire. She wriggled her right arm free from Lefty's slackened grip while he was distracted. She took hold of the reins and kicked the horse with fervor to get it running. In the confusion she managed to land a punch on his jaw—Lefty lost his balance and fell off his horse. He cussed as he regained normalcy after he got back on his two feet, but by that time Violet and his horse were far from his reach.

She turned the palomino appaloosa around and rode back with all speed to the hanging tree.

Billy clambered to get back up, but he did. He shimmied out of the lasso and pulled it over his head, and dropped the heavy rope on the dirt beside him, it thudded as a cloud of dust sprang up around it. Jasper was still on the ground, but managed to bound back onto his left foot. He groped with his large hands at his saddle while blindly searching for his pistol holstered somewhere there.

Billy could see Violet in the distance riding, alone, towards him. Jasper was too engrossed in finding his weapon to notice the lone rider barreling up fast behind him. When she reached

Billy, he swung himself onto the saddle. Jasper's blood boiled as they rode away.

Violet and Billy rode back into town, desperate to find some method of escape before Lefty or Jasper could try something else again. Lefty had been thrown from his horse fifty yards away from his gun. If he was still determined to secure the reward money he might follow them into town. Jasper's anger was that of a cornered and wounded beast.

Violet's only usable hand fumbled as she tried to untie the bandana over her mouth. Billy put her hand down gently and untied it for her and let it fall to the ground.

"Thanks. It feels nice to talk again." She smiled, relieved. Billy handed Violet her pistol, and she took it with a respectful nod. "Glad it could have some use."

She stayed outside the hotel on the appaloosa. Billy ran up the back stairway, and through the open door of the hotel room. He rushed to collect their belongings: saddlebags, his bedroll, Violet's gun belt, and his Henry rifle being chief among them. He could hear the clock in the room ticking as he left. It occurred to him that he hadn't paid for the hotel room. He ran down to the lobby, Maggie was not there, he dug several silver dollars out of his pocket put them on the guest book and left. To his relief Violet was still there. He ran over to the livery stable to retrieve his mare.

The adrenaline was beginning to wear off for Violet, and the pain in her ribs and shoulder returned to her. She had amazed herself with what she had done to stop Lefty—she had saved Billy's life and freed herself.

She now had a horse, but it had been stolen. She tried to justify stealing it, because it was a bad man's horse. She told herself that the fine appaloosa wasn't worthy of its former owner. Out of the corner of her eye she saw someone standing outside by the saloon doors, it was the bandido. That muchacho seemed to appear at the worst of times.

"What are you doing here?" Violet questioned. She was still not willing to trust someone that tried to kidnap her just the day before.

"I, señorita? I have helped defend you from the gunmen. Are they still alive?"

"Yes, but they might come back."

The bandido's eyebrows lowered in concern. Billy rode out from the livery stable on his horse. He recognized the bandido.

"Thank you, señor." Billy said, "To tell the truth, I wasn't sure if I could trust you at first."

"That is alright. I am a bandido… we are not famous for being trustworthy. The pistoleros might be coming back, no?"

"That's right." Billy replied.

"I can take you to a place where they will not find you." The bandido made two clicks with his mouth and from the alley on the far side of the saloon walked out a pure white mule. "My village is about twenty miles south of here. You can get supplies and rest."

"Gracias, señor." Billy said, "What is your name?"

The bandido held his chin up as he answered, "It is nothing. They call me Fortunato—the lucky one. What is your name, vaquero?"

"Billy Colton." He figured that if he was going to ride with a bandido he could drop his alias.

"Mucho gusto." Fortunato said.

"Mucho gusto." Billy replied.

Violet was apprehensive, she still distrusted Fortunato although he appeared to have helped them, but she hadn't witnessed it first-hand. Billy was less worried about it; he had a more open, trusting nature than his traveling companion. Fortunato smiled and looked at Violet. She thought he was trying to be too friendly, too soon. She responded by turning her head and looking away. She could not become friends with someone who had tried to kidnap her, even if he was helping them. She would not dignify him by telling her name. She was not one to forgive past offences readily. She looked Fortunato over and she noticed the bandages over the shotgun wound. Perhaps he had only helped them for revenge—if that was the case he could turn around any time and stab them in the back. She didn't know what his motives were in helping them, but she knew that she did not trust him. What other choice did they have? Lefty may still want to collect his blood money, and Jasper his revenge. There was no other town before Fort Concho and San Angelo for several more miles. Lefty and Jasper would not expect two gringos to be hiding out in a Mexican village. It could be the diversion that they needed.

Fortunato sat in the saddle of the white mule and motioned them to follow.

"This way amigos." He whistled to get his mule moving.

Their horses galloped until they were a safe distance from the town, but then they slowed to a walk to keep their animals from tiring. Fortunato led the way about fifteen feet in front of the small group, whilst Billy and Violet rode side-by-side.

"Do you trust him?" Violet asked Billy quietly as not to draw Fortunato's attention.

Billy looked thoughtful for a moment before responding, "I don't trust him, but I think he is true to his word..." he paused a moment before continuing, "I kept the truth from you, Violet. I saw him ride into town last night. I paid for him to get fixed up, so he could tell me who was following us."

Violet's mouth hung open as she stared wide-eyed at Billy. He continued, "I'm sorry, I know I shoulda told ya, but I didn't want to worry you badly."

She didn't know what to say. Touched by his concern for her emotional well-being in her distressed state, but also irked that he believed she couldn't handle the truth. She wished that he would have warned her about the danger from the gunmen, that way she might have prepared, and could have prevented capture by Lefty. Now she was in this mess with the bandido. Things were not going according to plan.

Violet spoke brusquely, "Can you please inform me the next time my life is in danger?" She backed her pony away from Billy.

Billy hung his head. He had managed to disappoint her yet again. He felt he could never get things right around her, although he desperately wanted to please her.

She knew she might have been too harsh, but she wanted him to understand that she didn't want to be kept in the dark about anything.

It was only mid-morning and the sunlight slanted across the prairie. The morning dew had evaporated in the heat of the sun. The humid air made Violet's hair curl and expand. Earthy smells rose up from the prairie sod. Violet was glad to be out of doors again, although she was in pain. Being shut indoors made her feel trapped. She wondered what Fortunato's village would be like. The impression that she had received from the bandidos was less than stellar, but she was willing to keep an open mind about the others.

Billy looked back at Violet. He was learning how to discern her moods. He could tell that she was nervous by the way that she was looking around and clutching at the reins. He thought about speaking some words of comfort or encouragement, but none came to mind.

By now Billy had switched from wearing the grey bowler, to his brown, wide-brimmed felt hat. He was grateful he had it too—the sun seemed to shine brighter and hotter each day. His mind wandered to thoughts about Fortunato's village. Were there more bandido's like him? Would they be friendly?

The little bit of Spanish he knew he learned from Gustavo. Gustavo was his father's ranch foreman. He was a caballero from Mexico, and one of the best riders north of the border. He hoped the knowledge he had of the language would come in handy.

# Chapter XII

Billy looked past Fortunato and glimpsed the first signs of the pueblo. There was a large, imposing gate with attached adobe walls. The gate was graced with two large pecan trees, one on each side. Peeking from the top of the wall was a mission tower with a tarnished brass bell in the chamber that looked like it had been there since the arrival of the first Spanish missionaries to the area.

"This is my village... Puerta de Chana." Fortunato said as he puffed up his chest. He shouted to a man in Spanish who was standing on the wall. The man ran down from the walls and soon the rusty hinges of the ancient gate creaked and the three riders were allowed inside the village. They had their horses walk through the main street of the town. It was quiet, but there were a few villagers purchasing supplies from the small open-air market. Scattered onlookers stared at the two gringos led by the well-recognized bandido.

"I will take you to my casa; my sister Lupe makes fabulous frijoles refritos." Fortunato said.

"What's that?" Violet whispered to Billy.

"They're refried beans—mighty tasty." He responded. Her only reply was to wrinkle her nose in disgust.

Fortunato led them up to a comfortable adobe house on the outskirts of town. It sat at the foot of a granite hill, sparsely spotted with trees and scrubby vegetation. There were horses, mules, and burros hitched outside a barn. The house had a large covered wooden front porch lit with several hanging lanterns. One man with a large straw sombrero had been standing on the porch. He rushed inside once he saw Fortunato.

Violet was tense and felt like she was being pushed into an ill-fated situation. Staying at a bandido's hideout might implicate her and Billy even further as outlaws if they were discovered.

There were shouts of joy from inside the house, and several men came out onto the front porch. The hombre with the straw hat shouted, "Fortunato! You are still alive, we thought you were dead for sure!"

"No, mis amigos... but many of my compadres have fallen." Fortunato said, as he took off his hat and let it hang close to the ground.

"Oh, no." The man in the straw hat replied, "The others are muerto?"

"Sí, amigo. It is a tragic loss."

The amigo patted Fortunato on the back and said, "But you Fortunato are always lucky…" He paused as he took notice of Violet and Billy. "Who are your friends?"

"The man who is trying to kill him killed all of my men, and almost killed me too." Fortunato gestured emphatically at his stomach where he had received the shotgun wound. "He also saved my life."

The man in the straw hat nodded to Billy but then eyed Violet and the horses. Fortunato turned around with a smile and motioned Billy and Violet to come inside. They hitched up their horses at the barn and walked into the house. The heady smell of beans welcomed them as they entered.

They were led to a long table made of thick wooden planks. A woman who had an uncanny resemblance to Fortunato, perhaps his sister, was holding several dishes full of food. Lupe was wearing a white dress and had her black hair worn in a long, thick braid. She gave her brother a nettled look as she struggled to put more food on the table for two extra bedraggled guests. Fortunato motioned them to sit. Billy pulled up a chair for Violet, and he sat himself down next to her.

"Thank you Billy." she said quietly to him and smiled. She was always impressed by good manners in men, although she wasn't always keen to admit it.

Fortunato and the man in the straw hat sat down as well, and began talking boisterously in Spanish. Billy struggled to catch a few words from their conversation here and there, and Violet could understand none, except for the expressions they were making which indicated that Fortunato was retelling the encounter with the gunmen. The man in the straw hat was much heavier set than his compadre, with a double-chin and a thick upward-curling mustache. He was also more loud and emphatic in his gestures.

Food was dropped onto their plates by Lupe.

"Gracias, señorita." Billy said.

Violet didn't know what to think of the mysterious brown paste on the corner of her plate. These must be the refried beans. She didn't want to be rude to the scrambling hostess, so she took a timid bite. She was pleasantly surprised by the smokiness of the beans and that they smelled and tasted much better than they looked. She took an even larger forkful. Billy stared at her in disbelief, he thought she wouldn't eat them, let alone enjoy them.

"Good ain't they?" he said smiling.

Violet didn't want to talk with her mouthful so she nodded forcefully. She ate the sauce-covered enchilada on her plate, and wondered how she could have not known that this wonderful food existed.

Violet felt someone's eyes upon her, she looked up. It was the man in the straw hat. She disliked the way he stared at her—he assessed her like she was a piece of property, and it made her nervous. Once they were finished with their food, Fortunato smiled and told them about their accommodations.

"There is a room that you two can have on the upper level. There are nice beds and Lupe can fix it up for you. Sí, hermana?"

Lupe rolled her eyes in response as she put a pile of dishes on the kitchen counter.

"Gracias!" he said in an attempt to appease her.

She just rolled her eyes again as she began scrubbing the dishes.

"Thank you again, Fortunato. Much obliged to yer generosity." Billy said.

"It is no problem, señor. The enemy of my enemy is my friend, no?" he said, laughing, "You can stay as long as you want. It is no trouble at all."

One could hear the slamming of the dishes in the kitchen as Lupe was getting more and more upset at the excess of generosity displayed by her brother.

"We'll be heading out soon, I s'pose." Billy said, trying to defray the anger of Lupe.

"Whatever you need is alright with me." Fortunato whispered so his sister wouldn't hear.

Billy nodded, but Violet was still uncomfortable with the situation, and especially with the man in the straw hat.

"Oh! I forgot to introduce my friend. We call him Armando."

Armando raised his chin and eyebrows abruptly in greeting. Violet got the sense that this man was somehow the boss of Fortunato. Why else would he hold such a large presence in Fortunato's home? She was curious about Armando, and about how the whole operation worked. Did he receive most of profits from the bandido's plunder? She didn't like Armando's look. There was something very unappealing in his eyes, something evil. The spark in them was not from God.

She couldn't help but agree to the lodging arrangements. She was injured and needed a sheltered place to rest her wounded bones; even if the only option was a bandido's hideout.

She was tired. The rush of escaping Jasper and Lefty had given her temporary zeal, but now she acutely felt the pain of her injuries and overwhelming exhaustion filled her body. Billy didn't look so good either. He had scrapes and cuts over his face and his pants and shirt had tiny gashes and tears in them from his body being dragged full-speed from behind a horse. She had enjoyed her food, but soon she felt pain in her stomach from eating too much too quickly.

Billy was chatty. He carried on conversation with the bandidos as long as they were topics that could not implicate either party. Violet was already tired of people and conversation, her one desire was to rest. Soon the conversation had quieted down, and most of the men were finished with their food. Lupe appeared from a long absence.

"I hoped you enjoyed your food. I am lucky that my sister is such a good cook." Fortunato said and volunteered his sister once again, "Will you show them to their room por favor?"

She led them up the creaky stairway and to their room. It was small and loft-like with a large window facing out to the stables. There were two beds, one in each corner, they were low to the ground, and to Violet's pleasure they had plush feather mattresses. She turned around and thanked Lupe. She nodded and shut the door.

Violet wanted nothing more than to rest her tired body on one of the soft beds but she remembered that their gear was still on their horses. "Billy, can you bring our gear inside? I'm afraid I need to rest."

He suddenly understood her motivation and left the room to retrieve their belongings. She thought that they couldn't be too careful, even if the bandidos had been friendly. She heard a quiet knock on the wooden door.

"Come in." she said.

Lupe peeked her head through the half-open door. She was holding a bundle of white cloth. She shyly walked up to Violet. "Your skirt... it's ripped. Here is another dress for you." She handed violet the white dress with red and blue embroidery around the edges. Violet had forgotten how torn up her dress had become. Her skirt had been reduced to rags.

Violet didn't know what to say. Perhaps she had misjudged the character of the bandidos and their families. "Gr-gracias." She smiled and took the dress. Lupe was pleased with her reaction and left the room.

Violet struggled to put the dress on with one arm in a sling. She untied the sling and the wide neck came over her head easily. She managed to tie the sling again with her one hand and her teeth. She let her hair loose from the bun that had been piled on the top of her head. Billy returned with his arms full of gear.

He was surprised to see that she had changed. She looked so natural and beautiful with her hair flowing down in front of the white wide-necked dress. He searched for something pretty to say but all that came out was, "You look like a girl!"

At first her eyebrows were raised in surprise, but then the corners of her mouth rose in a smile. She laughingly said, "I'll take that as a compliment. I reckon it's better than looking like trail dust."

They both laughed. She recognized that this was the first time she had really heard Billy laugh; his laugh was warm, thick and rich like honey.

Once they stopped laughing she got onto more serious matters, "Have you gone through your belongings to be sure everything is still there?"

"Everything's accounted for."

"I'm just concerned because we are in a house of thieves."

Billy furrowed his brow in contemplation. He did not share in her distrust of their hosts.

"While it's still light outside I'm gonna scope out the market they have down there." Billy said,

"Maybe they'll have a pistol I can use fer the time bein'."

He was angry that Jasper had just tossed his pistol aside. It had been given to him by his father who it had been issued to in the War against Northern Aggression. More recently it been used to shoot rattlesnakes, and old bottles and cans, before it had returned to its intended use. "Will you be alright all by yerself?" he asked.

"I'll be fine. Here…" She placed her pistol in the palm of his hand. "Take this until you can get another one." He tried to put it in his holster, but it was too big for the smaller gun.

"You keep my rifle with ya. I'll be back soon." he said.

Billy left the room and Violet laid down on the bed with the rifle beside her. She tried to sleep but the pain from her injuries made it difficult.

When he was downstairs he told Fortunato that he was going outside. Fortunato nodded, and Billy left.

The street was dusty, but it had a pleasant scent. The open-air market seemed to sell just about everything under the sun. There was a booth for each of fresh and dried fruits and vegetables; dried red peppers and garlic were strung from the ceiling, like aromatic banners. There were dry goods, beans of every color, and rows and rows of maize. There was a man selling miniature guitars and wooden flutes. An old Navajo woman was selling silver jewelry inlaid with turquoise and coral, which were nestled among colorful woolen blankets. The whinny of burros could be heard from outside an adobe stable, their masters eager to sell. Billy imagined this is what Mexico must look like. He kept walking to the end of the street and saw a small shop with a sign that read 'Fusiles y Pistolas'. He assumed by the word 'pistolas' that this was the right place, and stepped inside.

The building was small and cramped. The guns were laid out on a counter, and some on the wall. Among the weapons were flamboyant and finely worked leather scabbards, belts and holsters for vaqueros. There were also many small and large knives and swords, many of which had seen action from the Mexican-American War and the War Between the States.

He wondered how much a reliable pistol would cost. He had never had the need to purchase one for himself before. He saw many old Confederate issued handguns, stamped with the mark CSA on the handle. He shuddered at the irony that his old gun might have ended up in this very shop. There was a particular revolver that caught his eye. The chrome glinted brightly. It had a carved ivory handle that depicted an eagle with wings spread. He picked it up and handled it. It had a nice weight and feel and the grip fit his large hands nicely.

"How much for this one?" he asked the lone salesman behind the counter.

The salesman nonchalantly pulled on his thin mustache as he thought of a sufficient price, "Thirty dolares."

Billy set the revolver down like it was hot. He had never heard of one thing costing so much in his life. Added to this, he only had one twenty dollar gold piece which he had set aside in the case of an emergency. He continued to search through the array of pistols. There was another one he saw, not quite as flashy, it had a smooth black handle, but it was cold to the touch like ivory. He was intrigued by its uniqueness among the wood, hard rubber, and ivory handles. The metal was black and was blued from use. He asked the salesman what the handle was made of.

"Buffalo horn, señor. It is very beautiful, no?" The clever shop owner tried to increase its desirability to his customer.

The black gun was .44 caliber, the same as his old pistol. It would be nice not to buy a different size of bullet.

Billy took Violet's smaller gun out of his holster and set it on the counter. The shop owner's eyes grew large as he appraised the ivory handle and detailed filigree on the chrome.

"That is a fine pistol. Do you want to make a trade, señor?"

"Sorry, that gun ain't fer sale." Billy said as he tested the black-handled gun's fit in his holster, "How much do you want for the black one?"

The shop owner knew he was interested and placed his price high, but not too high so that his customer would refuse the gun outright. "Twenty-five dolares, señor."

Billy bit his lower lip as he tried to assess his financial situation again, and weighed his desire for the gun. He had paid a lot for the hotel and Violet's visit to the doctor that he only had his twenty dollar gold piece and ten whole silver dollars remaining for the whole trip.

"Ten dollars." Billy said.

"Twenty-two dolares."

"Fifteen dollars."

"Twenty dolares, it is a rare beauty."

"Eighteen dollars." He looked the salesman in the eye, indicating that this was his final offer. The salesman squinted one eye. "I will give it to you for nineteen."

"Alrighty then…" Billy set the pistol back on the counter, and began to walk away.

"Fine, I shall give it to you for eighteen dolares señor. That is all I can do." The salesman said as he put his hands up in a show of exasperation.

"Done." Billy smiled jubilantly. He handed the salesman the twenty dollar gold piece. The salesman opened a locked box on the counter and pulled out two Mexican silver dollars and placed them in Billy's hand.

"Gracias, señor." Billy said, tipped his hat and exited the store with the black-handled beauty.

# Chapter XIII

Violet's exhausted body had succumbed to sleep. Normally she didn't afford herself the luxury of resting during the day, but now that she was injured it was a necessity. She would wake up with pain riddling her ribs and shoulder. Her mind was still half-awake as her body slept. Thoughts and memories from the day bounced around her head like billiard balls on a table. If her body could have tossed and turned it would have. In the back of her mind there was always Jasper and Lefty. There was the question if Jasper would still give chase with a lame foot. Lefty was a loose-cannon, he seemed like he would do just about anything to claim his reward money.

During bouts of waking, she thought of O'Leary. He did not seem like the heroic sort, although he did ride away when he felt like justice was not being served. O'Leary's actions showed some strength of character that she was surprised to see that a hired gun possessed. She didn't dream, her sleep was too disjointed to allow it.

Billy stopped outside the front door to load his new gun. Like Violet said, it didn't hurt to be too cautious. Billy walked back in and found Fortunato and Armando sitting at the table with several other men. They were talking quietly, but he could not tell what about. Fortunato's normally friendly manner was gone. His thin black lines for eyebrows knitted together, "Hola mi amigo." Fortunato said, "I see you have found a new gun, huh?" He smiled as he looked at the gun in the holster.

"Sí, I got it from the shop in town."

"It is very nice—it fits you, señor."

Fortunato turned back to the table and his friends continued to speak to him. Billy had never felt suspicious before about the bandido, but now he could sympathize with Violet. There was something shady about Armando he did not like. Fortunato seemed different, there was a light in his eyes that his compadre did not possess.

Billy went back upstairs to check on Violet. To his relief, she was asleep. He opened up his saddlebag and took a swig from the bottle of Jim Beam because he knew that it was lost on his female travelling companion. He set the bottle down. He watched her sleeping, and he was glad she was getting some rest.

Although his body was fatigued, he was not tired yet. He was too agitated from the events of earlier that day. He caught a glimpse of himself in a small mirror as he was about to leave the room. He ran his hand over his roughed-up face. There cuts, scrapes and bruises on his jaw, cheekbones and forehead. As well as a deep crimson gash across his nose. Beneath the mirror was a basin and pitcher where he washed up. The water stung his dusty wounds, but it was soothing at the same time. He forgot to bring a razor with him, or else he would have shaved, for he had several days' worth of stubble on his jaw.

He walked back downstairs and Fortunato grabbed ahold of his arm as Billy passed by the table, "We are going to have some music tonight," he said, "my friends Alejandro and Gabriel will play guitar… and my sister may sing.".

Billy hadn't had much entertainment for what seemed like an eternity. A little bit of music seemed just right to calm his weary soul.

Fortunato continued, "If you want, your friend could join us."

"Much obliged," he replied, "but I reckon she won't be joining us."

He took a chair from the table and placed it against the back wall, and tipped his hat over his eyes. He pondered how he got into this precarious situation in the first place. Soon he drifted off into a thin sleep.

Billy was awakened by the hollow sound of guitars knocking against the wooden table. Two men were sitting in front of the table, and they each held a gut string guitar. They were ready to play for their friends. Lupe was still in the kitchen. Billy could only see her when she peeked out from behind a wooden column. Armando stared at her possessively while he smoked a pipe in the dining room. Billy sensed that Lupe was uncomfortable with Armando, or perhaps just shy, Billy was never quite sure of what women were thinking.

With a few flicks of their wrists, Alejandro and Gabriel began playing a light flamenco number. The magical sound reminded him of nights around the campfire on the trail, when the ranch foreman, Gustavo, would break out his guitar and sing to the cows. Billy missed his family and the ranch. The ranch had been his whole life—until now.

His father had done well. Henry Colton, or Hank, as he was known, came from Illinois as a destitute young man. He had heard the tales of Texas, especially those of its rich, almost inexhaustible supplies of land. He held tight to his lofty dreams, and they spurred him on to success.

During the Civil War his father volunteered for the seventh Texas cavalry. Billy, not even a man at fourteen, was forced to take care of the ranch as soon as his father left to fight. Soon the ranch became his life. During the dark days of the war Gustavo, the ranch manager and Hank's best friend, became like a second father to Billy. He struggled because he had an urge fight against the Yankees, but he had a responsibility to his father and the rest of his family. He grew up working hard, and playing hard at the end of it, and that is what he knew. He was lucky enough to see his father ride home safely from the war. Since then they ran the ranch with the help of Gustavo, some hired hands, his younger brother Paul, sister Junie, and his mother. At the present time they had 10,000 acres of fine Hill Country grazing land.

Billy was knocked back from reminiscing by a more up-tempo number from the guitar players. Fortunato was in the kitchen begging his sister to sing for his guests. Billy couldn't hear anything, but he saw Fortunato motion with his hands toward the dining room. Lupe was obstinate and refused several times before she took off her apron, threw it on the floor and entered the dining room. She stood in front of Alejandro and Gabriel and prepared to sing. She had a rich contralto, and she sang with a 'who-cares' kind of attitude. Billy could understand only a few words as her voice dipped and scooped the Spanish phrases. He could tell it was a love song, but a sad one. Most Mexican love songs were sad. He noticed Armando staring at her while she sang, trying to catch her eye, but she turned away every time he did. She was singing it for herself, not for anyone else.

Billy thought about waking Violet up so she could experience Lupe's singing. He stopped himself as he remembered that she was seriously injured and needed her rest. He watched Lupe's face as she sang, and it was full of alarm— something was wrong. He turned to his left where Armando had been sitting, but he was gone. Fortunato was still sitting to Billy's right, but another onlooker was gone. He got up with a start.

"Where is Armando, Fortunato?" Billy demanded.

Fortunato looked shocked and worried, "I do not know señor."

\* \* \*

Violet could not sleep any longer. The pain in her chest and shoulder was too great, and she decided a walk around the room would do her good. She looked out the large window and saw something terrible. Armando and an accomplice were riding Billy's mare and her newly acquired appaloosa, along with two other horses away from the stable. They were booking it from Puerta de Chana with great speed. Hot anger flowed to Violet's face. Those two horses were the only means of escape for her and Billy. She had been used, and she would never trust a bandido again.

# Chapter XIV

Billy ran out of the adobe house to ascertain Armando's whereabouts and to check on the horses. The stable gates had been flung wide open, and all that was left inside was Fortunato's white mule. There was no sign of his brown quarter horse or Violet's palomino appaloosa. He turned to Fortunato who was now beside him. "Where are the horses? Where is Armando?"

Fortunato was dumbfounded, and stammered out, "I-I do not know, señor… perhaps he will come back."

"Come back? What do you mean he'll come back? He's a bandit! That was my only horse!"

Billy threw his hat on the ground, incensed. He picked his hat back up and stomped into the house and up the stairs. Violet stood in the room still gawking from the window. She looked at Billy with wide desperate eyes, her mouth hung slightly open from shock. She couldn't imagine things being much worse.

"The horses are gone…" she said in disbelief.

"Armando took them." Billy said, tight-lipped.

Her eyebrows lowered over her dark eyes. "I know. I knew he was no good."

"Damned bandit stole my horse,"

"There's no way to catch up to Armando now…"

"You're right. How are we going to get out of here, and get you to San Angelo?" When Billy voiced the question he remembered that Maggie told him. "There's a stage coming Monday morning in Deer Creek."

"Do you think it's safe to go back there?" Violet questioned, her voice wavering.

"Jasper's got a lame foot, I reckon he won't 'spect us to be back in town."

"What about Lefty?"

"I don't know. He might be crazy enough to hide-out and try to bushwhack us. All I know is I ain't got a horse and neither do you. We've got to find some other way."

"I suppose we don't have enough money for two new horses." She sighed. "How much do you have? If you don't mind me asking."

"I've only got twelve dollars left, used most of what I had to buy this here pistol."

She rubbed her eyes in worry. "I only have forty dollars, which is not nearly enough for two good riding horses, not to mention saddles and tack."

Billy bit his lip, as he realized that his precious saddle and tack were gone forever. He bought them last year after the last big cattle sale, and had his initials specially monogrammed into the leather.

"Couple of bastards... excuse my language miss."

Violet just ignored his apology because she was just as upset as he, and if it were acceptable for a lady to swear she would have. A cramped stagecoach is not what she had in mind for her transportation in San Angelo, especially since they were now wanted. He waited for her to say something.

"We really have no choice, I suppose we should start heading back towards Deer Creek." she said.

"Will you be alright walking?"

She gave him an incredulous stare, "I *am* an Indian, and we did walk before we had horses."

Billy chuckled and said, "Alright."

Fortunato entered the room, unwelcome. "I am so sorry compadres! I had no idea that Armando would cheat you."

"Sure you didn't." Billy challenged him. His guard was up like quills on a porcupine.

"It is the truth, señor. I did not know he would steal your and the señorita's horses."

Billy turned around to face him. "I heard you talking to him, Fortunato."

"We were not talking about that, señor. I would not have had him steal from my guests." he pleaded.

"I don't believe you."

"You must believe me, señor. Armando is a very powerful man. I do not know why he stole your horses. You should not cross him."

"Fool me once, shame on me. Fool me twice, shame on you. I ain't gettin' fooled twice by you Fortunato."

Violet stayed silent while she sat on the bed. She wanted to stay out of the argument.

Fortunato tried to repair his reputation and continued to beg for forgiveness. "I am sorry, señor y señorita. Please, stay in my house for the night."

"I will not accept any more of your charity." Billy picked up both his and Violet's saddlebags and flung them over his broad shoulders, along with his sheathed Henry rifle and his bedroll. Billy walked out of the room. Violet didn't know what to think, but she followed him down the stairs.

"Are you sure this is the right thing to do?" she asked.

Billy looked her in the eyes. "He broke my trust. I won't stick around here if I don't have to." He paused. "Will you be alright?"

"I'll be fine." she responded.

"We're gonna head back to Deer Creek, hopefully in time to catch the stage."

Lupe appeared from the kitchen. "Please, forgive my brother. He means well, but it does not always work out. Armando is dangerous. I pray to the saints that you can get back to where you need to go." She then mumbled a few words in Spanish as she crossed herself.

"Thank you." Violet said. Lupe slipped her a cloth-wrapped bundle of flour tortillas.

The sun was already low in the sky, it wouldn't be long until the first pink and orange colors of sunset would appear in the west. They began their march toward the town that had given them so much trouble earlier that day. They had only gained about a mile on the rough and rocky terrain before they stopped for the night. The sun was glowing red orange on the horizon, and they had to make a fire fast. There was a chill that the cloudless sky brought and Violet could tell it was going to be a cold night. She began gathering small sticks for tinder with her only operable hand. Billy insisted that she sit down, and that he would build the fire. He continued to search for brush and larger sticks of wood. He knew he had several more matches in his matchbox, and as dry as it was out there anything would catch fire quickly. He picked up several rounded pink granite rocks and created a small fire ring. With one strike of a match, soon the fire was blazing.

"I'm sorry, Violet." Billy said with shame in his voice as he gazed at the crackling flames.

Violet looked up, somewhat surprised by this. "What are you apologizing for now?"

"I feel like this whole thing is my fault."

She was even more shocked by this most recent statement. "What do you mean Billy? You did not know he was fixing to steal our horses."

"I reckon you're right..." He dubiously said as he threw another stick on the orange fire.

Violet pulled out her Indian blanket and tried to unroll it.

"Here, let me help you with that." Billy said.

"I've got it." she insisted.

"I know you do." he said, leaning over her. He laid it out nice and pretty on the ground, "It would just have taken you a coon's age."

Violet smirked, "I reckon I should say thank you."

"You're welcome."

Billy laid out his bedroll next to hers, because it was the only flat piece of ground next to the fire. He pulled out his harmonica and began playing a tune that was unfamiliar to Violet. She listened for a while to the cheerful melody, until her curiosity was overpowering. "What is that song you are playing?"

"It's called the Yellow Rose of Texas."

"It's pretty."

Soon Violet fell asleep to the sound of Billy's harmonica. Sometimes it was better not to travel alone.

Once he noticed that her eyes were shut he stopped playing and crawled into his bedroll with his rifle next to him. He woke up twice in the night to add fuel to the fire and to make sure no intruders were near. Once, he awoke to the wail of a lone coyote. He noticed Violet shivering and loaned her his blanket. He wished to high heaven that she could have somewhere nice and safe to sleep. A seed of doubt grew regarding his decision to leave the comfort of Fortunato's dwelling.

* * *

The doctor took his pair of small surgical scissors and cut straight down the shaft of Jasper's enormous black boot.

"Those are my best pair of boots!" Jasper exclaimed in anger.

"I figured you won't be needing them anymore," the doctor said, "They already have a hole in them."

Jasper's eyebrows lowered over his dull eyes. He let out a dog-like yelp as the doctor attempted to remove the lead bullet from his foot.

"What the hell did you do that for?"

The doctor shrunk back. "I have to remove the bullet."

Jasper huffed and slammed his head back angrily onto the leather operating chair cushion. Lefty was standing next to him watching the gory scene take place.

"What are you gonna do with the bullet once you get it out?" Lefty asked, eager-eyed, as he chewed open-mouthed on a chaw of tobacco. The doctor just raised one eyebrow in response. He examined the wound, and many of the bones in Jasper's foot had been shattered, the bullet was lodged deep within his flesh. He knew that the foot would be useless for the rest of his life.

The doctor handed him a bottle of whiskey, of which several gulps were swallowed. The doctor pulled out a pair of long tweezers and carefully extracted the small piece of mushroomed lead. He pulled it up to his spectacles and then dropped it on the tray table. Lefty stared at the bullet and his hand hovered toward the tray table.

"Do you want me to keep the bullet for you, Jasper?" Lefty asked.

"Hell no!"

The doctor gave Lefty a disapproving sideways glance, and Lefty withdrew his hand. The doctor rinsed the foot off with whiskey and then bandaged it up.

"Try not to walk on it," he said matter-of-factly, and continued, "I wouldn't advise riding either."

"Dammit," Jasper growled under his breath.

"Do you want me to get your horse for you, Jasper?"

"Get away from me you dunce," Jasper said as he pushed Lefty away with his gigantic left arm.

# Chapter XV

Billy stoked the fire, there were several glowing red coals still burning. He searched through his saddlebag for something to eat. He pulled out the tin of biscuits, he was grateful that his mother had had the foresight to give them to him. He grabbed the percolator and began to make coffee with some water from his desert canteen. He worried about using the water for a luxury such as coffee, but he knew that Violet would appreciate it. There wasn't a creek or source of water anywhere nearby. It was a good fifteen more miles back to the town of Deer Creek. When they had ridden their horses over this terrain they had not seen anything that looked like a suitable water source. He hoped that Violet would be alright travelling on foot, and that their water would last.

Violet began to stir with the smell of the coffee. She opened her eyes and saw Billy next to the fire, she smiled. It was a comfort to know that she wasn't totally alone in the wilderness. She stopped herself from smiling too much—she didn't want to take too much of a liking to the cowboy. She tried to get up from the uneven ground using her right arm for support, it was difficult as hell with her other arm in a sling and the burning pain coming from her ribs. Billy reached out his hand and grabbed her right arm and pulled her up. She tried not to blush.

"Much obliged." she said once she was settled, and wiped the dirt off her skirt.

Billy didn't say anything in response to her offer of thanks, "Would you like a biscuit and maybe some coffee?"

"I would love a biscuit and some coffee." She smiled.

Billy handed her a dented tin cup full of the hot brown liquid. Her hair was wavy and damp from the morning dew. She had inherited her mother's German hair.

Billy didn't eat or drink anything until she finished her coffee. He handed her the last biscuit. He noticed that his stash of biscuits was dwindling much faster than if he had been travelling alone. He grabbed a handful of jerky from a burlap sack to satiate his hunger.

"Here," Violet said as she handed him the flour tortillas. Once they had finished their breakfast Billy started to pack his things up.

"Are you ready to head on out?" he asked, legitimate concern on his face.

"I'm fine," she responded, "stop worrying about me."

She kicked off her boots and pulled on her moccasins. She packed light, and it allowed her to put items away if necessary, like her boots. Billy helped her up again and began to roll up her Indian blanket and stuff it away. She was angry because she felt so helpless, it was not normal for her to rely on others for support. At the same time she was grateful to him because it would be nearly impossible to accomplish some of these simple tasks if she were alone.

Billy slung each of the saddlebags over his shoulders. This was going to be rough country — full of twist-leaf yucca, juniper that clung to life with their white, bare-bones branches, and thorny mesquite trees. The land was crisscrossed with dry and rocky creek beds that hadn't seen water for several months or even years.

Violet was still angry with Jasper Smith. She cursed his name under her breath for being a filthy, lying, rat. This anger somehow motivated her to walk even faster and farther to accomplish her goal of getting to San Angelo. He had tried to kidnap her and kill Billy. But she wouldn't let Jasper stop her.

She was glad to have her moccasins, because she seemed to walk better in them than her clunky riding boots. In fact, she was walking faster than Billy. She slowed her pace because she didn't want to out-distance him while he was carrying both his and her saddlebag—that wouldn't be polite. She may have been injured, but there was nothing wrong with her legs or feet.

Billy brought his eyes up from the rocky earth. Violet was ahead of him and he marveled at the pace that she was keeping. He thought he would have outpaced her. He learned at that moment to never underestimate Violet.

The sun waxed higher in the sky, and was just beginning to display its midday brightness and heat. Violet was beginning to realize the toll her injuries had taken on her, and she slowed down. It was more difficult to maintain her balance over rough terrain with her arm in a sling. She had forgotten how much one uses their arms while walking. Billy was by her side and keeping up with her for the first time since they had started. She stayed silent because she was concentrating on keeping her balance.

"Do you have any brothers or sisters?" Billy asked.

"Yes, I have one little brother, his name's Luther. He's about sixteen." Violet said. She stopped walking, and raised a hand to her sweating head. "I think I need to stop and rest a spell."

She sat down underneath a juniper tree. She hadn't realized how hard she had pushed herself. Her scalp was throbbing, and her heart was pounding from the heat. She was so focused on getting to her destination she had forgotten to ask for anything to drink. She hadn't had enough water.

Billy could tell that Violet was dehydrated, and possibly suffering from heat exhaustion. Most people were not used to the intense Texas heat.

"Here take a drink." he ordered her as he handed over his canteen. She only took a few gulps and tried to hand it back to him. "No. We'll get more water. You're going to get sick if you don't drink up."

She reluctantly drank several more ounces. She looked down through the narrow mouth of the canteen, it was almost empty. How were they going to find more water? In Missouri one could practically fall into a stream while one was walking if one wasn't paying attention, but not here. This land was dry and unforgiving. The only moisture present was the humidity in the air.

She was amazed by the hardy people living in this land. She thought of the Apache that had forsaken their lush, mountain home in Canada to live here, and the white settlers that carved out thriving ranches, businesses and towns. It seemed to get drier and drier the further west she went.

"You should take it easy for a while. You don't want to get tuckered out." Billy said as he sat down on a rock beside her, "I'm plum wore out." He pointed to a roadrunner scampering around the rocks. "El Paisano—they're supposed to be good luck." He smiled broadly. Though it was just a silly superstition, it did bring some comfort to her weary heart.

# Chapter XVI

Violet trudged on. The soles of her feet began to ache. Billy was only a few paces behind her. There was sweat on his brow from the toil of carrying both of the saddlebags. The intense heat from the mid-day Texas sun added to his misery.

He admired Violet's tenacity and courage. Time and again she proved that she was no ordinary woman. She was made of tough stock—the kind that survived and carved out a living on the frontier. Billy realized that he only had one or two swallows of water left in his canteen. They needed to find a source of water quick, or they might both suffer from the effects of dehydration, heat stroke, or worse. Water was more valuable than gold under the Texas sun.

His eyes searched the ground for any indication of water. He hoped to find a dried-up creek bed, or if he was lucky a fresh puddle of water. It was a fool's notion to believe that there would be flowing water in an arroyo this late in the summer, especially in brush country.

His keen eyes spotted a row of brush that was just a little bit greener than the surrounding brown flora. The greenery was flanked by a shallow ditch full of reddish granite sand.

He called for Violet to stop. He let both of the saddlebags slip off his shoulders and fall to the ground. He frantically dug with both hands. They were well suited to the task, he had wide palms and sturdy work hardened fingers.

Violet watched him in bemusement. She could not understand why he was on his knees shoveling the dry sand like a dog.

"Come here!" he called again.

Violet reciprocated and went to the shallow ditch. The ditch was wide and twisted like a snake off into the stands of mesquite and juniper trees.

"What in the name of Sam Hill are you doing?" she asked.

"I found an arroyo, or what you might call a dry creek bed. Gustavo, our ranch foreman, taught me how to find water when we got lost searching for a couple strays. You never know when you might be ailing for water." He half-smiled in self-satisfaction.

He had only dug about eight inches down and the sand was still dry as a bone to his disappointment. He clawed at the sand even faster. Just a few more inches down and it became dark and heavy. He rubbed the moisture laden grains between his fingers.

"Just a little bit farther and we may strike gold." he said as he looked up at Violet. He continued to dig. He scooped out the wet sand with care onto a separate pile. "We might need this for later."

He wiped away the sweat that dripped from his face with his shirt sleeve. His brow furrowed as he became concerned that the life-saving liquid might never present itself. He continued to dig even faster. Water rushed from the earth into the hole which was now a foot and a half deep. He smiled a full-toothed grin of triumph. Violet was impressed, but she didn't show it. He had proven to her that he had skills that even she did not possess.

There was soon a puddle of brown water. There was at least enough for two people to drink. Billy rummaged through his saddlebags— throwing things out until a dented tin cup appeared. He dipped it into the silty water and put the cup to his lips for a taste. He nodded.

"It's good enough to drink." he said as he handed the cup to Violet. She took a sip of the water. It tasted fresh despite the slight sandy mineral taste and opaque light brown color. It had come from a source flowing underground and had been filtered through thousands of pink granite grains of sand. It was as wholesome a water source as one would find in the dry brush country. The water soothed her dry throat and seemed to flow to her tired muscles, invigorating them.

"Thank you." she said as she placed the empty cup back in Billy's hand. He filled his cup with water from the hole and bottoms-upped it. He filled his cup again and poured it carefully into the narrow mouth of his tin, wool blanket covered canteen. Violet grabbed her leather bota bag and handed it to him so it could be filled as well.

As she watched him fill the canteens she couldn't help but notice how ruggedly handsome he was. His jaw sloped like a hill flecked with brown stubble. His eyes were as bright and clear as the Texas sky. They were different than the eyes of those she loved—different than the deep emerald green reminiscent of Missouri woods in spring. These eyes were open and full of innocence, not like the deeply wooded mystery of Cyrus's eyes. Billy's full bottom lip glistened from just having drunk the water. If it were a different time perhaps she would have kissed him—or maybe the heat was getting to her causing her to have mad delusions.

Billy pondered their current predicament. He seethed with anger toward Armando and his patsies for stealing his most valuable possessions—his sturdy ranch quarter horse and saddle. He was angry with himself for trusting Fortunato, a known bandit. If he could have punched himself across the jaw, he would have. He had made the best choice based on the circumstances, but his best was never good enough, and that killed him. He toyed with the idea of tracking down his horse, but he dismissed it as impossible. How could he find one stolen horse out of the tens of thousands of equine that were in Texas? Why didn't Armando rob them outright and take their guns and money? He didn't know. From his experience with Violet, he had learned to trust her instincts about people. He could tell that she was uncomfortable around Armando, and Billy disliked the way he had stared at her, like a hungry wolf stalking a wounded lamb. He couldn't let the anger of the past consume him. He had to concentrate on getting Violet safely to Deer Creek and on the stagecoach to San Angelo.

"Are you ready to go?" he asked Violet.

She looked at him with her dark almond shaped eyes. "I think so."

"We're not exactly in a hurry, so if you want to rest we can." He waited for a moment, but she didn't respond, so he took that as permission to get going. He slung the saddlebags over his shoulders, and handed Violet her bota. They continued northward toward Deer Creek.

The isolation and silence of their journey

caused Violet to ask herself how she came to the Texas brush country, injured, and travelling on foot with a good-natured cowboy named Billy Colton.

She had left her home in Southwest Missouri on a lark. By her family and friends Violet was known as a cool-headed, practical girl, but she had a stubborn streak and an adventurous spirit which could not be tamed. Something more powerful than any other force in the universe had spurred her on her journey across the wooded hills and open plains of Indian Territory, and finally down to the wild frontier land of Texas.

She had encountered and conquered loneliness, fear, dangerous persons, and the elements. She had experienced more on her lonesome than she had travelling with her new-found companion. She was beginning to think that he attracted trouble, like a magnet.

These last few days had been particularly trying. Her mettle had been tested in more ways than she could have imagined. Her painful injuries made her realize her vulnerability. She was not, as she would have liked to believe, invincible. Their emotional toll seemed to outweigh the physical one. She was not accustomed to being sick or injured. Most frequently she was the one that volunteered to tend to others. She was not often on the receiving end of charity. Trusting herself with an almost complete stranger was out not only out of the ordinary, it bordered on the impossible. She had learned even as a small child never to trust anyone. She had learned hard lessons due to prejudice regarding the color of her skin and frowned-upon mixed heritage.

One of Violet's activities as a child were the trips to the general store with her mother to buy penny candies. The bell atop the shop door rang as they entered, her mother holding her hand. Violet could see jars on the counter holding the colorful striped candies just out of her reach. She wanted the pink and blue one. As she let go of her mother's hand an old woman in the corner spat in front of her small feet.

"Riff-raff shouldn't be in here. Little half-breed creature, it ain't fit to be born!" The old woman said through crooked yellow teeth.

Violet cried and ran back to the safety of her mother, hiding behind her mother's large skirt. She couldn't remember what happened after that, but she remembered her mother swearing in German. She and her mother left so quickly that she never got her candy. That day she became conscious of the fact that she was different, and often-times despised for it.

Billy was different than the others—she had

learned to trust him with her life in the span of just a few days. He had been kinder to her than just about anyone she had known. That gentle kindness reminded her of someone else she knew; someone whose face was etched in her memory.

She recalled that fateful day when that letter arrived in the mail. She had ridden into town to fetch some supplies from the general store. She had taken special care to wear her dark green plaid dress with her white bonnet, since going into town was a special occasion. As was her custom, she swung by the post office to pick up the mail. She hoped deep down in her heart of hearts that she might receive some correspondence from the one she loved. She had not heard from him since the end of the war. Last she heard from him he was a cowboy—driving the wild Longhorn cattle from Texas up the Goodnight-Loving Trail to the Union Pacific Railroad town of Cheyenne, Wyoming. From there, the cows were packed into train cars, and sold for more than nearly ten times their worth to hungry mouths and deep pockets back East.

She sifted through the usual business letters, most addressed to her father, and then came across a small envelope with strong, fine, tidy script addressed to Miss Violet Corntassel. She hastily turned the envelope over for the return address; her heart was beating out of her chest. It was written in tiny letters on the reverse, Cyrus P. Morgan.

With shaking fingers she pried the glue from the paper and pulled out the letter. She read it on the spot.

My Dearest Violet,

It has been too long since I have seen your beautiful face. I have secured a job with a Mr. Freeman. I continue to work driving cattle. After this year's herd is sold I plan to purchase a fine plot of land of some five hundred acres. You can acquire land for pennies here! Texas is the most splendored place that my eyes have ever beheld. I hope, my dearest, that you may see it someday. Soon I will have amassed enough wealth to build a fine house and start my own ranch.

I fully intend to keep the promise that I made before my departure. Unless you have stolen the hearts of other beaux! Come to Texas, my dear, and then we shall be married.

Yours Truly,
Cyrus Morgan

His signature was stately and flowed elegantly. It reminded her of his character which was manly, yet refined. She was overjoyed at the news that he wished for her to come to Texas. She wanted to shout at the top of her lungs. Finally she would have her own life. Finally she would be with the one she loved.

Now all of this was brought upon by a bright promise made long ago, when she was still quite young. She remembered the night that she sat alone in her room and waited. Violet bit her nails. Her mother always told her it was a bad habit, but she didn't want to stop, especially since she was so nervous. It wasn't quite dark yet, just a few more minutes until she would see the first star appear in the velvet-blue sky. He had told her to meet him by the old cottonwood tree on the road between the two properties. Her heart fluttered as she thought of him. He was tall, and twenty years old. He had pitch-black hair, dark as a deep southern night. His eyes were green like emeralds in sparkling wells. She got lost thinking about him. It was dark enough, and time for her to leave. She sneaked out of the front door. Her father was reading his newspaper with his eyes half-shut. She tip-toed, holding up her calico skirts so they wouldn't rustle and let her father know what she was doing. By now she knew all the wooden boards in the house, which ones creaked, and which ones were quiet. She did the painstaking dance of stepping on the right boards to get to the door. She made sure to oil the front door-hinges earlier that day so they wouldn't squeak as she left. Carefully she turned the doorknob, making sure that it was silent. Swiftly, yet quietly she slipped out the door. She ran, petticoats in hand, to the old cottonwood tree.

She remembered the first time she had seen him, when he came with his father to get a new horse. He saw Violet standing on the front porch, in her bare feet, she was embarrassed and ran back inside and put on her moccasins, it wasn't the custom of girls to show their feet in public. He smiled at her and she painted that smile in her mind. Later they officially met at the town box-social. She had never loved someone so much. She was only fifteen but she was swept away in love.

It was a warm summer night and the smell of honeysuckle hung sweet in the air, perfect for a tryst. She could see the cottonwood tree, and there he was, as tall as a church steeple. In the moonlight she could see his gleaming smile beneath his pencil mustache.

"Cyrus!" she said as she ran into his arms for an embrace. "I waited until it was dark enough to go outside."

"Violet," He smiled again, "I wanted you to meet me here tonight…" He swallowed as he seemed to try to think of the right words to say. "I've loved you since I saw you standing there barefoot on your front porch." His long thin hand slid into his pocket and pulled out nail bent into a ring. "I'll be leaving soon, and I know it's not much, but I'll get you pretty one with a real diamond as soon as I get back." He paused for a moment. "Will you promise to wait for me Violet?"

This was the moment she had waited for.

"Yes I promise." He slid the make-shift promise ring over her finger. "It's perfect." She pecked Cyrus on the cheek. "I have to go… they'll know I'll be missing soon. I love you." she said has she released both of Cyrus's hands. She turned around and blew him a kiss as she giddily ran back to her house. She could think of nothing but the happiness she felt at that moment. Her mind wandered to girlish imaginations about her future. Soon the dark shadow of the war would take him away from her.

Suddenly she was torn from her daydream, and thrust back into harsh reality. She had stopped walking, and Billy stared at her, sufficiently confused.

"Are you… alright?" Billy asked.

The truth was that she wasn't alright. She hadn't seen her intended in such a long time, and all she wanted was to be with him. A storm of emotions rushed over her. She felt sadness, loss, joy and love at the same time. She started walking again, but this time at a faster pace. She wanted to walk the sadness away. Moisture formed in her eyes, and seemed to rest heavy on her lower eyelids. She looked up at the sky to prevent fat tears from running down her cheeks. The sooner she would get to Deer Creek, the sooner she would get to the stagecoach, San Angelo and then to Cyrus.

\* \* \*

Jasper Smith sat alone at the end of the long bar. He downed another shot of whiskey into his gullet. His large, sausage-like fingers formed into a fist and slammed down onto the counter, which startled the bartender and the saloon patrons.

"Get me another round." Jasper said.

The whiskered man tending bar put another shot glass in front of him along with the entire bottle of Jim Beam whiskey. Some patrons stared wide-eyed and open-mouthed at the large stranger with the bandaged foot.

"What the hell do you think you sons of

bitches are lookin' at?" He scanned the room, and none of them responded. He went on to insult the entire room, "I thought so…"

Jasper pulled out the small regulation Confederate pistol from his britches and examined it like it was a piece of precious metal. Hatred seemed to gleam in his eye as he looked at the bartender under a dark brow.

"Do you know what this gun is?" Jasper said in almost a whisper.

The old man gulped, "No,"

"It's the damn pistol that shot me in the foot, that's what!" The decibel level rose from a whisper to practically a scream. He tucked the pistol back into his britches. "And the damned son of a bitch who shot me with it, is gonna pay."

The bartender nodded in fear, here was a very large, very drunk, heavily armed man in front of him making death threats. He continued to wipe down the counter, but kept his sights on the sawed-off shotgun in a cubby just below the bar, just in case.

Jasper drank his last shot of whiskey and limped outside to his horse. Lefty was standing there holding the reins.

"Here's your horse, Jasper."

Jasper wiped his nose with his shirt sleeve and fell into his saddle. The horse began to trot off out of town towards the east.

"What are you doing, Jasper?" Lefty asked.

"Goin' home." he bellowed.

"What about me?"

"Get yer own damn horse. You're the one who lost it... to a woman!" Jasper broke out in uproarious laughter.

# Chapter XVII

Billy and Violet made camp near a grove of pecan trees. The setting sun made the cedar covered butte and rolling hills glow red. Billy helped her unroll her bedroll. He made beans for supper, but Violet wasn't hungry. She was too tired and weak to want food. She just laid there and stared up at the dusky sky. She reminisced over happy times she and Cyrus spent together, and the dreams they had. Her one hope and wish was that those dreams would come true. Deep within her soul she yearned. With all that she had been through she felt it nearly impossible for those things to come to fruition. She felt ill when she thought that she might never see Cyrus again. The last time she saw him, she thought he might be gone from her forever, to be lost to the tragedy of the war.

The Captain stood with the 17th Missouri cavalry under the magnolia trees outside the Morgan manor. He had a dark handle bar mustache and wore his grey cavalry cap low on his stern forehead. The Stars and Bars was held high, and seemed to glow in the cloudless sky. It flapped violently in the wind. Cyrus stepped out of the double doors and the sunlight shone on his Confederate grey uniform. His family was one of the few wealthy enough in the county to afford him one. The sparkle in his emerald eyes was dim. He said goodbye to his father, mother, his younger brother, and three sisters. They stood on the large porch complete with white Grecian columns. Violet stood by the side of the brick mansion and watched out of sight of his parents.

The Morgans came from an aristocratic clan in Virginia. Chauncey Morgan (Cyrus's father) uprooted his small family west to Missouri after he was disinherited by his father. Seemingly because of a scandal that spread like wildfire through the parlors of Virginia. He rebuilt his reputation and his empire from the ground up.

Cyrus's and Violet's promise of love had been made in secret because his parents severely disapproved of her Cherokee father. They could never stand to allow the son of the wealthy Morgan dynasty, and heir to the plantation to marry a half-breed. They passed off his relationship with Violet as childhood foolishness. But she knew otherwise. After the farewells had been made to his family, he sought out Violet. Her wavy hair flowed gracefully in the wind. She ran up to him, at this point she didn't care about being seen by his parents any more. This was the last time she would see him until the War Between the States was over... or something else happened.

She dreaded the thought as she looked into his eyes. "I'll miss you terribly Cyrus." she said.

"I know."

"You'll promise to write me?"

"As often as I can."

The captain of the regiment called for him to join the cavalry.

"Goodbye." she said, in a soft whisper.

His mother's shrill voice shouted, "Go Cyrus, or they'll leave without you." Her grey eyes shot a furious glance at Violet.

Cyrus looked back at Violet as he rode away with the cavalry. She waved to him frantically, put on her best smile and blew him a kiss. Bittersweet tears welled up in her eyes—she never imagined love could be so painful. She watched until Cyrus disappeared over the horizon, and she prayed within her heart that she would see him again.

She ran to the house, trying to hold back a sob. She closed the front door quietly, as not to disturb her family. Her father was reading his newspaper (as usual) at the small kitchen table.

"Say goodbye to Johnny Reb?" he said.

Violet quickly tried to hide the tears by wiping them away with her apron.

"H-How did you know?" she stammered.

"I'm your father, I know everything." His wise face half-smiled. "Saying goodbye is difficult, but we must trust that we will see them again. Your mother made soup." He winked and continued to read his newspaper. There was the familiar smell of her mother's strong German potato soup coming from the large pot hanging in the fireplace.

"Vat are you telling de child?" The mother called from the kitchen.

"Nothing, dearest."

"Zoup will be ready in a minute liebchen. Go fetch your little bruder."

She went to the field behind the house and grabbed her little brother. He was just eleven at the time, and he had been hunting for rabbits with a slingshot in the tall green grass.

"Ma made soup. Get in here." She grabbed her little brother by the arm and led him inside. "Hey! I almost got one Violet, I don't want any soup."

She replayed that day in her mind and it was as vivid as if it happened yesterday. She was taken back years later to that fateful day when she received correspondence from Cyrus.

After she read the first letter, she continued to search through the small stack of post. There was another letter from Cyrus, but the handwriting was different, it was scrawled and messy as if it had been rushed. She opened it with urgency and began to read. To her horror there were drops of dried brown blood splattered on the upper right corner of the page.

> Dear Violet,
> I have taken ill. There was a dispute between another gentleman and myself that ended in gunfire. I hope my last letter found you well, for I still wish for you to come to Texas, and urgently. The doctor does not relay happy news to me; he says that in my weak state that I have contracted pneumonia. The one thing that brings me joy is that I might see your beautiful face again.
> Yours truly,
> Cyrus Morgan

The signature was his, but scrawled and messy, dwindling out on the last letter as if he had lost the strength to write. Violet was in shock, she never expected to hear that Cyrus had been shot. That fear lingered within her during the war, but she thought he would be safe during a supposed time of peace—if reconstruction could be called peace. The letter trembled like a leaf tossed in the breeze in her hands. She imagined the pain a gunshot wound might have caused, and she could almost feel it in her bones. She went over to desk and asked the woman when they had received the last letter from Cyrus.

"Just this morning, ma'am." the desk clerk replied.

"Thank you."

Violet rushed out the post office doors and clambered onto the uncovered buggy. She snapped the reins with a great yell and the horses ran like bats out of hell.

She arrived back home to the small cabin where she had grown up. She began to gather her things for her long journey. She wanted to be with him. She wished she could be at his side in an instant. She would try her best to get there as soon as she could. Deep in her mind she knew it would be an arduous journey. The farthest west she had ever traveled was to the eastern portion of Indian Territory, but she wouldn't let a petty thing like distance get in her way.

She fumbled about her room and in a panic, packed all the things that would be necessary for a trip of over seven hundred miles. First were the precious letters tied with yellow ribbon she had received from Cyrus during the war and beyond. Second was the food, all she had in the cupboard were a dozen or so dried out corn pone cakes and beef jerky. She ran out to the garden and picked several ripe, juicy purple tomatoes and stuffed them in a burlap sack. She went through her clothes, her large hoop dresses and petticoats wouldn't be appropriate. Her eyes went over her split riding skirts; she grabbed the brown pair, and a white shirt, as well as a pair of well-worn moccasins for comfort. She pulled on her knee-high leather riding boots. She buckled on her spurs, her father had gotten them on a trade with a man from Mexico.

Her gun belt and holster hung on a hook in her closet, last used for shooting cans during target practice. On her nightstand lay her 1859 Remington Rider, with ivory grip and filigreed gunmetal, which had been converted to house bullets instead of lead balls. Her father had given it to her as a birthday present a few years earlier, for personal protection while she was out riding. She would need it again. She slung the leather gun belt, straight-draw, around her waist.

From her nightstand drawer she took her life savings of gold and silver coins, held in a small leather pouch. She grabbed her wide-brimmed, dusty-grey felt hat off a hook on the way out of her room.

She went into her father's room and pulled out a pair of canvas trousers, and a floral printed dress shirt from his dresser. Luckily her father was on a horse-trading trip, and might more easily forgive her once he knew the situation. She took the time to scribble a note. In it she informed her father and brother of her departure, that she was going to Texas to see Cyrus. She promised further correspondence in the future. She signed it with all her love, and kissed it before she laid it on the table.

She went outside and filled her water bladder to the brim from the stream flowing nearby her house, and filled another larger horse canteen. She was almost ready to embark. She walked past the horse corral to the stables. She needed a horse with tenacity and spirit to take her on such a difficult journey. There was quite a selection to pick from, her father being a horse farmer and trader. As she walked through the different stalls she passed by quality roans, blacks, and bays. When her eyes came upon the small, pinto mustang, she knew he was the one for the job. He was spirited, and was caught not too long ago from a herd of wild horses. He was already saddle-broken, but still stubborn. He went in circles, whinnied, and turned away from her, as she tried to land her saddle on him. In the end he cooperated, and Violet settled into the saddle. She flew off along the trail in a flash of chestnut and white.

She stopped her horse for a moment on the crest of a hill and turned around for one last look goodbye to the place she knew so well. The small cabin stood like a beacon of her past. Her memories seemed to have been absorbed by the sturdy wooden logs. It represented her family, and the only real home she had ever known. She might never see them again. The sun shone across the wooded valley, and seemed to light up the terrain in a celestial blaze. The hills, trees and streams were sketched in her mind. In the East was her past. She turned away and looked out West, toward her future.

# Chapter XVIII

The next morning Violet woke up to a dusty scent rising up from the earth as she shifted in her bedroll. She rubbed her eyes. She had not expected to fall asleep while reliving a moment of her past. It was still early, and the sun had not yet fully risen over the horizon. The coals from the fire the night before still had a few burning embers left in the dark wood. Billy was still asleep. She contemplated making a pot of coffee, but the water would be put to better use on their journey back to town.

She searched through her saddlebag with one hand for something to eat. She pulled out a large can of peaches. Nothing sounded better to her than fruit at that moment. Not often did she have canned goods on her long-distance journey. It would be impossible for her to open the can with one hand. Thankfully Billy woke up by himself when he heard her rummaging through her supplies. He looked confused, as if he should still be asleep.

"Good morning!" Violet said cheerfully as she handed Billy the can of peaches.

"What's this?" he said.

"Peaches, I can't get to them with one arm." It was as good as if she had asked him for help.

Billy pulled out his bowie knife and stabbed the top of the can.

"We're not that far from Deer Creek." Violet said as she looked northward.

"How can you tell?" Billy asked as he looked up from his work.

"I remember this grove of trees." She pointed to the stand of pecan trees behind them, "We should be less than two miles from town."

"Don't move." Billy said with his eyes as wide as saucers.

"Why, what's…" Violet said. His expression turned to steel as he reached for his pistol and seemed to point it right next to her. "What are you doing?"

There was a loud bang, Violet jumped. She turned around to see what he had shot. It was a small black, yellow, and red snake with a thin head.

"Coral snake," Billy announced, "they'll for sure kill you—more dangerous than a rattler."

"I've never seen one before…" was all she could say.

Billy kicked the dead snake off the blanket, which had already set into rigor mortis.

"Gun works." Violet commented, with nervous laughter. Billy smiled, sat down and opened up the peach can.

"Here ya go." He handed her the can of peaches. Violet ate one slippery yellow peach half.

"Do you think Jasper will be in Deer Creek?" she asked calmly, but Billy could see the nervousness in her eyes.

"I don't think so—shot him pretty good in the foot." He stabbed a peach with his knife and popped it in his mouth.

"Lefty seems like a wild one," she observed, "you never know what that type might do."

"It'll be alright." Billy said as he looked into her eyes.

He spoke as if he was going to make sure everything would be alright. She just hoped she could make it to the stagecoach on time and without another incident. This trip had been more difficult than she bargained for. She could only hope that it would end well.

They finished off the last of the canned peaches, broke down camp, and headed toward Deer Creek.

* * *

A familiar dark horse rode up to the Smith mansion. Jasper alighted his steed and limped into his brother's house. He dragged his large, heavy, lame foot through a chandeliered foyer, and rumpled the Oriental rug in the long hallway. He burst through the double doors of the office, and only half-surprised his brother who was sitting, jotting down numbers on a large piece of paper.

"What is the matter, brother?" James asked.

James had a well groomed van dyke and shoulder-length dark hair. He was a cleaner, lankier, and cleverer version of his brother.

"I need somebody killed." Jasper said through a clenched jaw.

"You know that I have already taken care of many of your embarrassing indiscretions. I hope you are not getting into any more trouble. I almost had to fend off an Apache raid, thanks to your *activities*." he said as peered with his dull brown beady eyes over a pair of thin, rectangular spectacles. His voice was as smooth-as-silk, and had demonic ring to it.

"Son of a bitch shot me in the foot—with this." Jasper slid Billy's pistol onto the paper-filled mahogany desk.

"I see..." James replied as he examined the standard CSA revolver in his hands. "Was this man Billy Colton?" he asked sharply.

Jasper's eyes widened in shock, "How did you know it was him?"

"I know about the little deal you struck with the Sheriff. You can't shield my eyes in this county." he said as he placed his spectacles on the desk. "Where were his last whereabouts?"

"Deer Creek, though I have reason to believe he is headed to San Angelo with a woman."

"What reason is that?"

"Hotel owner talks too much."

James eyed the pistol again. "I suppose you tried to have him dispatched at Deer Creek?"

Jasper nodded. "I can't follow him anymore..." He indicated that his lame foot and wounded arm were the issue.

James walked a few paces behind his desk with his hands folded behind his back. "I know a man named Edmund Forrester. He will handle the situation... He'll certainly manage better than your little hired guns."

"I got one request: I want Colton shot with his own gun." Jasper said as he pointed to it on the desk.

"Very well, I didn't know you were sentimental. I'll have it shipped to Forrester with the orders."

Jasper nodded once and then limped out of the room. James pulled out a small drawer from his desk and took out a map of surrounding Mustang Ridge. He studied the Colton's ranch and marked the boundary with a red pencil.

# Chapter XIX

Billy and Violet walked onward. Around noon they saw the first signs of Deer Creek. She thought it strange that they were returning to a place they had fled from danger just days before, which was now looked on almost as a sanctuary. Billy's hand hovered over the black buffalo grip of his gun as they walked onto Main Street. They passed the livery and noticed the empty corral; Mr. McCarthy had not returned. Much to Violet's disappointment they would still be forced to take the stagecoach.

She carefully observed every person she saw. The few people out and about were dressed in their best suits and dresses. She realized it was Sunday. There was something about travelling that made the days run together. Most people seemed to be on their way to church. She scanned each of the passers-by, neither Jasper nor Lefty were among them. But that was no reason to let her guard down.

She had not recalled seeing a church on their last visit, although it was brief, maybe there just hadn't been enough time. Her eyes were drawn to a saloon where whole families freely entered, including women and children, and the men took off their hats.

"Is that what I think it is?" Violet leaned into Billy's ear.

"I suppose so." he said, took off his hat and walked into the saloon. Violet followed him in. The stuffy room was filled with churchgoers, flapping palmetto fans to cool themselves in the sweltering heat. The tables had been pushed aside to make way for extra wooden chairs all lined up in rows, facing a portable pulpit. A few men took advantage of the bar stools facing the grey-whiskered preacher. There was no alcohol in sight behind the mirror-backed bar.

"That was the barkeep," Billy whispered.

"Isn't that a conflict of interest?" Violet whispered, "It seems a bit of a small house for the devil and the Lord to both reside within."

They filled some empty seats near the front of the congregation.

She was reminded of the times when she and her brother were dragged to church by her mother's strong German hands. Her mother was a devout Lutheran and wanted her children to grow up in the ways of the Lord. The church that they attended was small and the sidings were painted white. She remembered that the preacher spoke emphatically, but she would hardly pay attention to what he said and would much rather look at all of the women's baubled shoes and swaying hoop skirts, much to the chagrin of her mother.

Her father rarely attended church. He believed in the Christian God and the traditions of his fathers. God and the Great Spirit were one and the same to him. He was trained to be a medicine man in his youth and learned the great prayers and potions passed down by generations before him. The Cherokee way of life soon changed, and the whites encroached on sovereign Cherokee land. He was faced with a painful proposition: if he held onto his traditions he would be shunned and persecuted by the whites, and there would be no way to feed his family in this new white man's world. So he put away the ancient writings and became a horse farmer, so that no one would disrespect him again.

After her mother died, they stopped going to church.

Violet was jarred back to the present when the barkeep began his sermon.

"Good morning to you all. It's nice to see some familiar faces this Sabbath day." The preacher gave a sideways glance to Billy, "I will begin speaking from the book of Matthew in the New Testament. Now Jesus went up upon the mountaintop and began to preach to the people, and he said: blessed are the poor in spirit for theirs is the kingdom of heaven…" he continued through the different beatitudes, "Blessed are the peacemakers: for they—"

He was interrupted by a man who stood alone in the back of the room, his hat still on. He had a crazed smile on his face.

"May I help you son?" the preacher asked sullenly.

"Yes, you can get me a drink, barkeep." He spat out the last word.

Violet instantly recognized the voice as belonging to Lefty.

"I'm sorry, but the bar is closed Sundays. Today it is a house of God." the preacher said.

"A house of God?" Lefty laughed in disbelief, "I don't need God if I got liquor."

"I'm sorry son, I can't do that for you today. Why don't you join the congregation?" he pleaded.

"No. I ain't come for no sermon—I've come for a man named Colton." Lefty pulled out his gun and pulled back the hammer with shaking fingers. "I ain't leaving until you tell me which one of these sons of bitches is Colton!" There were scattered screams among the congregation, and mothers held tightly to their children. "I saw him come in, and you know it ain't right to lie…

preacher! I ain't afraid to start shootin'." Lefty waved his gun around the room.

"Now take it easy, son." the preacher said as he slipped his hand into his inside jacket pocket.

Billy pulled out his gun, twisting around while he stood up. Lefty had surprise and fear in his eyes as he faced his opponent. There were squelched yelps from the crowd, and many ducked down, prepared for a shootout. Violet pulled her gun out of its holster and cocked back the hammer.

Lefty's dirty finger began to squeeze back the trigger, now aimed at Billy, but before he could make off a shot a small ball of lead pierced him in the left side of his chest. He brought his hand to the expanding spot of blood and examined it with quivering fingers. He let out a little laugh. His eyes rolled back into his skull and he crumpled onto the floor like a rag doll.

Billy stood with his gun pointed to the ground, speechless. He uncocked the hammer of his gun and slipped it back into his holster, Violet did the same. The preacher stood with his small pea-shooter still in hand, but it was quickly pocketed. Billy looked at the preacher with a mixture of disbelief and gratitude. Violet didn't know what to think, she was relieved and disgusted at the same time. Relieved that Lefty was no longer a danger to them, and disgusted to see anyone die.

"Sorry about that folks. Y'all go home and take it easy for a while. We'll see to it that this misguided man is buried."

Two men dragged Lefty's body out of the saloon by his boots to the undertaker across the street.

Violet busted through swinging saloon doors and ran into the alley next to the saloon. She felt like she was going to vomit. She felt out of breath. She needed fresh air. She tried to take slow steady breaths, but it was almost impossible from the pain in her ribs. She was nearly recovered, and after a few moments she heard the saloon doors creak behind her. It was Billy.

His brow was furrowed in worry, and his blue eyes looked intently at her. He didn't say a thing—he didn't know what to say, so he just rubbed his hand up and down her upper arm.

"I—I just needed some fresh air, that is all."

Billy waited a few seconds before he spoke, "Are you gonna be alright?"

"I don't know. Things have been so—I didn't want things to happen this way." Her dark eyes looked up at him—moist with the onset of building tears. "I don't know how I'm going to keep going." she said in an almost-whisper, with her head hung low.

"You're tougher than prickly pear cactus. You'll do alright." he said as he smiled. That smile helped her more at that moment than any other remedy that could be thought of. Violet did something that she did not normally do; she grabbed Billy around the waist with her good arm and gave him a hug. He accepted, though he was in shock, and carefully wrapped his long arms around her.

"Thank you Billy," she whispered in his ear, and then pulled back, "for sticking with me."

"Of course," He smiled. "Come on, let's get outta here." he said lightly as he tilted his head in the direction of the hotel. He had only walked a few paces before he felt a hand on his shoulder. He turned around, startled. It was the preacher.

"I need to talk to you, son. I need to know why I had to shoot that man."

Billy looked at him open-mouthed for a moment. "I'm sorry about what happened... I didn't mean to start anything." he said humbly, he was at a loss for words, "That came out wrong."

The preacher looked at him hard for a moment, but then his eyes relaxed. "Why don't we go to my house and you can talk to me about it."

The preacher led them to a modest house on the end of Main Street. They walked in and then were invited to sit on a white striped sofa. The preacher sat on a matching chair facing them. Billy felt like he was in an interrogation. There was an uncomfortable silence, and the tick-tock from the clock on the wall seemed to sound like thunder.

"I'm just a preacher, not a lawman. Anything you say will stay in my confidence. I know your name is Colton."

"Yes sir,"

"Why was that man trying to kill you?"

"It's a long story, sir."

"I've got time, the service is cancelled." The preacher looked at him with penetrating eyes. He crossed his legs and folded his hands on one knee.

Billy began to explain his meeting Violet, the run-in with the Apache, Jasper Smith, the wanted posters, his innocence, and the attempts on his life by the hired guns. The preacher nodded.

"I see... Well, at least I know you're not a liar. Liar's don't make stories like that one up." He smiled a little, and then stood up. "Good luck Colton, you're going to need it." He shook his hand and showed them to the front door.

Billy and Violet walked back from the preacher's house to the hotel.

"Well, that was interesting." Violet said.

"What?" Billy asked.

"That back there. I was impressed with your story too." Violet smiled. She hadn't realized the scope of her incredible journey so far until she heard it spoken.

They walked into the hotel lobby. Billy noticed that the window that had been shot days before was now boarded up, and ready for repairs. He stepped in holding his hat, like a bashful little boy who had gotten into trouble. He was worried that they might be unwelcome. Maggie sat behind the reception desk.

"Well howdy. What brings y'all back to Deer Creek?" She seemed to be unfazed from the shootout on Friday.

"We were... visiting some friends." Violet said. It was the best answer that she could come up with, though she didn't consider Fortunato and the bandidos friends.

"I'm sorry about your window ma'am. I'll pay for the damages." He had a sheepish look on his face.

"Oh, fiddlesticks! My brother-in-law is in the glass business. Was it you they was shooting at, kid?"

"Yes ma'am."

"Well, then you've got no reason to be sorry. I'm sorry they was after you. My son Joe has had some *disputes* before, and I'm sure it weren't your fault. You seem like the good kind." She smiled and showed them up to their room.

Violet thought that this town must be used to shootouts, based on her recent experience at the church, and Maggie's cool countenance.

Billy and Violet got settled in their room, and then went downstairs to eat a lunch of thickly-sliced smoked ham, corn and beans. The homey smell filled Violet's nostrils, and she was grateful to have real, hot food again. Billy asked Maggie what time the stagecoach left town.

"They usually get going at the crack of dawn. This one is taking a chest of gold wages to the black soldiers at Fort Concho, but don't worry, they have a good shotgunner riding along—my son Joe." Maggie said with a smile.

Violet was so exhausted from days out in the heat that might have rivaled that of hell, so straight after lunch she crashed into bed and fell into a deep, weary sleep.

# Chapter XX

While Violet slept among the soft pillows and blankets in the generous bed, Billy did not sleep a wink. He sat up all night in the high-backed chair and watched the street from the window with his Henry rifle in his lap. Sometimes he almost drifted off, but he was too worried about what might happen if he let his guard down. He had experienced too many dangerous encounters over the course of this last week, things that nearly killed him or Violet. He learned that it couldn't hurt to be too cautious. Soon the grey light of dawn showed on the horizon. It must have been as early as four o'clock in the morning, since the stars were still shining brightly in the dark blue sky. The moon shone through the window, casting cross-shaped shadows from the window pane onto the bed. Billy wished that he didn't have to wake Violet, but he gently shook her right shoulder; her eyes blinked opened.

"Is the stagecoach here yet?" she asked, her voice still carrying the weight of sleep.

"It should be here soon." he said, still holding his rifle with both hands.

Violet sat up on the side of her bed.

"How was your sleep?" she asked turning to him.

"Fine." he said as he looked out the window for any sign of the stagecoach, or worst-case-scenario, Jasper Smith. Once she regained her bearings, Violet untied her sling. She rotated her wrist slowly, and then made a fist. It hurt, but not as much as before. She stuffed the sling in her saddlebag just in case she might need it again.

"What do you think happened to Jasper?" she asked Billy.

"Ain't been no sign of him."

"Lefty was alone in the church, I wonder why he had no one else with him." She stopped herself, "I reckon it doesn't matter…"

"I don't know. I just hope Jasper ain't no further trouble." Billy said as he stared out the window, he looked rather menacing with the light of the moon shining off the stock of his Henry rifle, Violet never expected to see him like that.

"Me too," she said.

Violet began to gather her things. She brushed out her hair with a wooden comb that had several chipped teeth. It had been a long while since she had brushed it, and the tangles in her hair formed into big knots. The waves in her hair were smoothed out little by little as she combed. She figured she could stay in the white Mexican dress so long as Billy was with her—no reason to dress like a man if she had a travelling companion. She stopped combing for a moment.

Would Billy be coming with her?

The thought hadn't occurred that he might not come with her until now. Besides, he had no real reason to go to San Angelo but to protect her. Was it necessary anymore? Certainly she would be safe with the other passengers in the stagecoach.

She recalled the first time she tried to dissuade Billy from going with her. She didn't want to bring up that sore subject again if she could help it. It was different this time—she actually wanted him along. When the passengers boarded the stagecoach she would know what his decision would be.

She heard the hoofbeats of several horses, and the creaking of wheels. Outside the window, she saw the Concord stagecoach ride up and park near the hotel with a team of six dark horses.

Billy gathered up the saddlebags and put his rifle in its scabbard. Maggie stood draped in a shawl in the lobby hotel to see her guests off. Billy paid her the hotel fee, and tipped his hat as he left.

The large words Wells Fargo & Company were painted, marquee style, in bright yellow on side of the coach on a panel above the small door. Violet couldn't quite tell in the dim morning light, but the stagecoach seemed to be painted bright red with yellow wheels. From the looks of it seemed to be a six passenger vehicle—apparently not too many people were itching to go to the distant frontier lands of West Texas. Standing beside the stagecoach holding the reins was a middle-aged man with a thick mustache, full beard, and a round beer belly. Next to him was a young man carrying a shotgun, who she assumed was Maggie's son, Joe. He had blond bushy hair, flipped out of his eyes and an innocent, crooked, school-yard grin.

"Howdy." The bigger man tipped his hat to Violet and Billy. "Where'll y'all be going to?" he asked, his lips curled around a large pipe.

"San Angelo." Violet said assertively.

"We'll be headin' in that direction." he said casually as he climbed up to the driver's seat. Got to stop at Fort Concho first, drop off these wages for that brunette cavalry… " The driver thumped the locked cashbox on top of the coach, it made a slight jingle. "What are you aimin' to find in San Angelo, ma'am?" the driver said, "It's a rough and rowdy place from what I hear."

"It's personal business." Violet said defensively. She knew that she could handle plenty of rough and rowdy places on her own.

"I see." he said, and raised an eyebrow. "Will that young man be accompanying you?" He pointed a round finger at Billy.

"Yes sir." Billy said clear as day.

Violet's heart jumped when she heard those two little words.

"Good. We got some more passengers coming along in a few minutes," the driver said, "if you don't mind you can sit and rest a spell before we set off."

Violet was glad that Billy was coming—he had really become her friend, but this also complicated matters. What was she going to tell Cyrus when she stepped off the stagecoach with another man? Worse, what was she going to tell Billy when she finally met Cyrus? Billy didn't even know the real reason why she was going to San Angelo. He may have come to some inaccurate conclusions, such as an inheritance, or some other financial or legal reason that required secrecy. He would have never guessed that her journey was for love.

She sat down on the wooden bench on the hotel's front porch. She would be cheating Billy if she kept him in the dark, especially since he had proven himself such a loyal friend. What would Billy think? Would it hurt him? She milled the questions around in her head, like a dealer shuffling cards in a deck. Billy walked towards her and sat next to her on the bench. He turned to face her.

"Are you ready to go to San Angelo?" he asked, trying to fill the time before they boarded the stagecoach.

Violet nodded once. She paused for a moment and looked down at her boots.

"Billy, I need to tell you something."

He nodded, and looked at her with his clear blue eyes. She hated to have to tell him something that might bring them pain.

"I need to tell you why I'm going to San Angelo."

Billy's ears perked up, and his eyebrows rose. He had been waiting for her to tell him since they met, finally the truth would be revealed.

"I'm sorry I didn't tell you sooner. I've had to play my cards close to my vest. You've been so kind in coming all this way with me, I feel that I owe you—more than that, you deserve to know."

She looked him in the eyes again, and for a moment she felt like she couldn't do it. A lump in her throat prevented her from speaking. A flashflood of emotions came rushing to her, her duty to a promise that she had made long ago, and her love for Cyrus. And there was a new emotion, the love that she had for Billy. He was the most loyal and kind friend she ever had, and he had sacrificed so much without the thought of anything in return. It pained her to break it to him.

At last she regained control of her voice, "I need to tell you before we arrived in San Angelo." She was stalling, she took a deep breath. "I have gone all this way to meet my fiancé."

Billy jerked his head back—that was not what he had expected to hear. He had thought perhaps a deed to a gold mine, or some sort of property out West, but a fiancé? He never thought about Violet having another man in her life, he had only pictured himself. He did not know what to think, his thoughts were frozen. He sat silent with his hands folded in front of him—shocked to realize how little he really knew about her.

He should've guessed that a woman as beautiful and capable as her would already be promised to another man. He felt naïve that he had ever loved her, he thought he had been so stupid to entertain his boyish hopes. Why would she ever return the love of a simple cowboy? He had given himself too much credit. He swallowed hard.

"Alright." he said as he looked her in the face.

Billy's response was calm, but in truth, he was not alright. As Violet met his direct gaze his eyes seemed somehow hollow, the usual light in his eyes absent.

"Now that you know, do you still want to come with me?" she placed the question.

"Sure. I told you I would go with you to San Angelo. I don't throw away a promise easy." Billy stood up and threw the saddlebags on top of the stagecoach.

At first he was shocked, but that cool shock melted into hot anger. Anger towards Violet, that she would doubt his intentions of sticking with her. Anger, that she never told him she had a fiancé until now. Anger, that she never trusted him.

Anger at this fiancé. He had never met the man before, but feelings of jealousy burned within his heart. He was jealous, and he couldn't believe it. He had never been jealous before in his life, because he never had a reason to care enough. There had been girls he had courted, but he never felt the need to fight to keep them. He had risked his life for Violet, because he loved her, and he doubted that any other man could feel the same way that he felt about her. He was not about to let her go now—but he had never really had her in the first place. He felt his heart sink into a deep, dark pit.

The smell of freshly brewed coffee wafted from Maggie's kitchen. Billy stood up and lumbered to the inside, hoping that a hot drink might do him good. He let the door slam shut behind him.

Violet sat outside, alone. She knew she had hurt Billy, but not to what extent. She felt guilty that he had developed feelings for her that she could never honor without being untrue to Cyrus. She had taken too much of a liking to the kind stranger. She tried to force Billy out of her mind. She had left home because of Cyrus, *he* was her fiancé, she had promised to marry him because she loved him, and she couldn't break the trust of something so sacred. She loved Cyrus, and he loved her.

She imagined that Cyrus had clung to the hope that she would come to San Angelo to be with him. She wanted to be comforted, for someone to tell her that she had done the right thing to tell Billy the truth. A stray tear fell on her white skirt, like a singular raindrop. She felt totally alone.

# Chapter XXI

The stagecoach swayed side to side like a baby's cradle. The sun had risen, and the new morning heat oppressed the passengers. Violet sat by her lonesome in the back corner of the compartment. Near her head was a leather-flap covered window, if it could be called a window, having no glass to protect the occupants from the elements. It didn't seem to serve much of a purpose: when rolled it let out some of the oppressive heat, but in exchange let in a fair amount of trail dust.

There were several other people in the stagecoach with her. They were all interesting in dress and person, Violet liked to ascertain these features and keep them in her memory like a postcard she could refer to. On the leather bench directly across from her sat a tall, lanky man with a thin handlebar mustache and long sideburns. He had a short-brimmed hat and a tawny plaid three-piece suit. He carried a small, black doctor's bag and a crate of medicine which had been tossed on top of the stagecoach. He always seemed to have a pleasant expression. To his left was a trader, a man bound for Santa Fe she reckoned. He wore a wide-brimmed hat, the crown decorated with silver conchos, and a Mexican serape; he carried with him a leather shoulder bag and clutched box of fine cigars under his leathery knuckles. His stare was both nonchalant and unsettling, his light eyes an ambiguous color. Next to him was a black woman, confined to a corner, like Violet. She had an air of elegance, and her bright honey colored eyes radiated this outward. Her black hair was tied up in a large bun; she wore a royal blue dress of fine material. On the seat next to Violet was a blonde woman with her son who appeared to be about four or five years old, whom she held tightly to her.

Billy chose not to take the extra seat in the stagecoach but to ride on top, with his rifle. He said it was to protect the passengers against a potential robbery, but Violet knew it was because he wanted to be away from her. He had not yet forgiven her. She tried to forget about the young man who sat directly above her.

She stared out into the openness. The terrain was flatter than it had been closer to Deer Creek. Along her journey through Texas she noticed the hills began to disappear the farther west she traversed. The trees had become sparser, the ones she saw stood alone like sentinels on the vast and lonesome prairie. The stagecoach was slow, slower than Violet would have liked. It seemed that if a man were to run beside it he would keep pace with it for several minutes. Her impatience and anxiety was palpable. This was the purpose for her setting off on such a long journey. She wished to be with the one she loved, and for her quest to be over. She stared out the window with head hung back and imagined Cyrus's face. She wondered if he looked any different, if the war had changed him at all. She could see his clear, sparkling green eyes and dark hair and his long oval sculptured face, and most importantly his charming smile.

What if he had died of pneumonia? But that thought was shoved out of her mind within a split-second. She couldn't fathom his disappearance from this world. It was too much for her to bear, and she would be moved to tears if she dwelt on the dreadful subject any longer.

Billy squinted as he tried to focus on the horizon, but he got bored. There were two other men on top of the stagecoach with him (not including the driver or the man riding shotgun).

He wondered why Violet never revealed the truth about her fiancé sooner. Was there something she was trying to hide? He didn't know. No matter how close he had become to her, it was never close enough, and she would always remain a mystery to him. He was still bitter.

He was beginning to hope that this mystery fiancé deserved the beautiful and strong woman

Violet was. If she was going to be with this man, and he didn't appreciate her it would be like him grinding a wildflower into the dirt with his boot heel.

Billy was fixed on staying true to his promise, no matter what happened, he would see her safe to San Angelo. He was not the type of yellow-belly to quit halfway down the trail. He told himself it didn't matter who she loved—he would always remain a man of his word.

It had been at least three hours of rocking back and forth in the stagecoach. The general silence of the other passengers afforded Violet the opportunity for sleep. She awoke suddenly by a scream next to her.

"Get away from my son!" It was the blonde woman, and if it were possible she held her wriggling child even closer. The woman across from her sat there stunned, with her eyes wide-open in surprise.

"I was just going to give him some food. I have some extra apples in my bag…" The woman said in disbelief as she searched for the apples.

"We don't accept no charity from niggers."

The woman across from her shrunk back, obviously hurt from this woman's comments. Violet couldn't stand to see this injustice. She had experienced herself that awful feeling of being despised because of one's race. Her blood ran hot to her face with indignation; she could no longer stay silent.

"She was just offering him an apple, ma'am." Violet said firmly and directly to the blonde woman. The blonde woman looked at her in shock.

"I suppose you don't have a problem with the darkies, then?"

"No ma'am." Violet said.

"Well, I never..." The white woman said, flabbergasted, "them darkies were the reason my husband died in the war." she said with a shaky lip, and sharply downward pointed eyebrows.

"I'm sorry for your loss. But this woman is not responsible for your husband's death. She was just offering some kindness."

"Let's all try to be reasonable with one another. We still have a long way to go..." The doctor seemed to verify Violet's statement diplomatically.

The trader sat back and chewed an unlit cigar in his mouth, and observed the situation silently with a bemused smile on his face. The blonde woman's spine eventually relaxed back into her seat, and her grip on her boy loosened slightly, though she still looked at the woman across from her with contempt.

The doctor tried to break up the harsh atmosphere. "My name is Doctor Colburn. How do you do?" He reached his long, thin hand out to Violet.

"It's a pleasure, doctor. My name is Violet." she said, and shook his hand.

"What is your destination?" He was trying to cleverly change the subject.

"San Angelo."

The doctor's eyebrows shot up, he too was a bit surprised.

"Good luck there. Like many towns on the far West frontier, it has its challenges. It is my destination as well. I hope to open a practice. Their last doctor met an unfortunate demise, hopefully I will have better luck with my patients." He smiled uneasily, and then said quietly and leaned toward Violet, "Good thing I have more than scalpels in this little bag." He winked warmly.

Her heart sank at the prospect of San Angelo having no doctor. How long had they been without one? Was Cyrus safe, and had he received the proper medical attention he needed?

The mood seemed to calm down a little in the stagecoach after Doctor Colburn's and Violet's conversation. The man in the middle introduced himself.

"They call me Jack."

"Nice to meet you Mr....?"

"Jack, just Jack."

Violet nodded, though she thoroughly believed it was an alias. The black woman in the corner spoke, though still in shock from her fellow passenger flying off the handle.

"My name is Clarisse Hopkins. How do you do?" she said as she reached across the compartment to shake Violet's hand.

"Pleasure to meet you, I'm Violet."

"Likewise, Miss Violet. I'm going to meet my husband in Fort Concho, he's an officer in the Ninth Cavalry there." She shot a sideways glance to the woman opposite her, and waited for what she might say. The woman across from her only sat silent as her face twisted into a scowl. If she wanted to be unreasonable and miserable the entire trip, that was her own fault.

"I'm Maybelle Hawthorne of Tennessee, going to stay with my sister in Tankersley. Though I find this flatland unbearable, it is my only alternative after my dear Jackson perished in the valiant War for the Confederacy."

The hoofbeats began to be farther apart in duration, the stagecoach slowed to a stop. A roomy ranch house had appeared to the right. Violet could see a man standing outside. He waved down the stagecoach, and planted his hands near the driver's seat when the lumbering mass stopped. She could overhear him talk, "Howdy! I got a team waiting for you in the corral, and breakfast is ready."

"Much obliged." The driver jumped down and opened the door on Violet's side of the stagecoach. His voice took on an authoritative quality as he addressed the passengers, "Alright folks. This is the only stop for the next thirty miles or so. Y'all better fill on up and we'll head on out. Breakfast is fifty cents. Mrs. Mueller will see you to it."

Violet could tell that the driver was experienced and probably went back and forth along this route repeatedly. A woman (who she assumed was Mrs. Mueller) led them into a large kitchen. There was a long table made of wooden planks in the center, most probably built to feed hungry ranch hands. There were various blue and red pots and pans piled up on the sturdy wooden shelves. She could see Billy out of the corner of her eye; he was behind her, and the last to enter the room. He pulled out a chair for her, and hesitated a little before he sat down on the opposite side of the table. A generous breakfast of sausage, biscuits and gravy was placed in front of him. Billy gulped them down like a hungry wolf. Violet didn't feel like eating, she took a few shabby forkfuls. She poked at the steaming mass of peppered, white gravy.

She wondered why the truth had hurt Billy so much. Was he really that in love with her to be jealous? She wasn't sure if she wanted to know, she was in love with Cyrus. Her heart tugged at her in two directions, and she didn't like it. She looked across the table to get Billy's attention, but he only looked at her in passing, and then looked down at his plate. Should she apologize? She didn't see much of a reason to apologize. She was right to keep her secrets. What right did he have to know?

She knew she was kidding herself. Billy had done more for her than she could ever expect from a stranger. Despite his flaws, he was the kindest, most devoted man she had ever met. She should have told him her secret earlier. That was the past, what could she do about it now? Nothing, it was too late. She hoped that she hadn't lost her friendship with Billy forever.

Jack seemed to stare at her more than usual. It wasn't menacing, it was like he was trying to fit pieces of a puzzle together. Clarisse was very friendly to her, and made polite conversation while they were at the breakfast table.

"My husband's been stationed at Fort Concho since the spring. It's good pay, but it is indeed so far away. Seldom have I visited him since I am mostly confined to the area around Austin. The most difficult thing is…" her voice quieted to a whisper and she leaned across the table toward Violet, "is reading his letters about the Comanche. They have so many struggles, and I pray to dear God every day that he'll be safe."

Comanche, when Violet heard that word it took her back to when she first met Fortunato. He was threatening to sell her to the Comanche. Whether that was a bluff or the truth she did not know. Perhaps Armando had already sold their horses to the Comanche. If the bandidos did indeed have trade with the Comanche, Armando and his gang could still be very dangerous. The sliminess of Armando's character would allow him to conspire with the Comanche, as long as he could turn a profit. Violet hadn't realized that she had been daydreaming, while Clarisse had been speaking to her the whole time, and she had to say something in return,

"I am doing something rather similar. I am going to meet my fiancé in San Angelo."

Billy shot a dark look at Violet when he heard the word fiancé, and then shoved another forkful of biscuit into his mouth.

"Oh, how lovely… Where did you two meet?"

"We met when we were children, in Missouri."

Clarisse smiled. "I met my husband in Louisiana, after the war. He was assigned to Fort Concho shortly after we were married."

The driver came into the breakfast room, clapped and rubbed his hands together. "Alright folks, we're almost ready to depart, so finish your breakfasts and pay Mrs. Mueller."

Violet only ate about one half of a biscuit, but still paid the full fifty cents into a small box with a slit on top. Violet thanked Mrs. Mueller, and went back outside. The surrounding countryside was strangely beautiful in its quiet desolation. She could see two far off riders on horseback bringing some cattle in. She breathed in the grassy air; there were hints of juniper and other herbaceous smells. She could understand why someone would want to live out here. It made her think of Cyrus. Had he saved enough to buy the ranch, or had his illness prevented him doing so? The answer to those questions, and more, awaited her in San Angelo.

# Chapter XXII

Violet wanted to tell Billy about the possible connection between the bandidos and the Comanche, but he climbed onto the top of the stagecoach before she could say a word. She couldn't risk shouting it to him, they weren't supposed to talk about anything having to do with hostile Indian attacks or robberies. The words 'bandido' and 'Comanche' in the same sentence would not go over well with the driver or the other passengers.

The doctor soon appeared and helped her and the other ladies into the stagecoach. She appreciated the help, because her ribs and shoulder were still in pain.

Violet could feel the tug from the horses moving the stagecoach, and they were on their way again.

Two more hours passed riding through the golden flatland. Maybelle's scowl began to slacken due to muscle strain in her face. Jack continued to stare at Violet, and it was making her feel uncomfortable. She couldn't hold it in anymore, and in the most polite way possible she asked him, "Why do you insist on staring at me, sir?"

He replied, unoffended and unfazed, "You remind me of someone." That was a good enough answer to satisfy her question for the time being. She let it go, and he glanced at her with less frequency.

Violet missed Billy's company. His presence was comforting to her, and he always had a way to make her smile and lift her spirits. She wished he would understand her motives for not telling him the whole truth sooner, and he would forgive her. She wondered how long this separation would last. Would Billy walk out of her life and never come back?

She poked her head out the window and looked toward the horizon. The dusty yellow trail seemed to go on forever. Up to her left she saw several riders on dark horses that were so far away they looked like mere blurs, mixed in with the surreal lines of a mirage. She could not tell if they were cowpokes or possibly the cavalry. They seemed to be riding towards them. Eventually she could make out hats on the riders, but still could not see their faces, or tell their exact number. Why would they be riding so near the stagecoach trail so far away from civilization? She hadn't seen a ranch house or fence for miles. Fort Concho was still about thirty miles away.

The mysterious riders continued towards the stagecoach at breakneck speed. She wondered if she should warn the driver, but she assumed that he was more experienced than her in these matters. She also didn't want to cause any commotion between her already tense fellow passengers. There were four riders, and they were close enough she could see their faces, but they were covered by bandanas. Was it because of the dust?

One of the riders stopped his horse in the middle of the trail, blocking the stagecoach. The driver pulled at the reins in a panic. The sudden stop made the passengers fall forward, Violet's head whipped backward. Panicked eyes looked around, trying to decipher what had just happened.

The mysterious rider hopped off his horse and stood between the team of frightened horses, and drew a pistol.

"Gentlemen, ladies... This is a hold up." He had a sophisticated, drawling southern accent smooth as whiskey, which was masked by the gravel of the West.

Joe, still holding the shotgun, was at a loss. If he fired he risked killing the horses, and with it their only method of escape. The other riders surrounded the stagecoach and pointed their firearms at the driver and the man riding shotgun.

"Put down your weapons and this will all go smoothly." The main man in front of the stage said. The men on the top of coach complied, except Billy whose hand slithered for the buffalo-horn handle of his pistol.

"I wouldn't do that if I were you, stranger. You've got three guns pointed at you on each side." The main man said.

Billy put his hands up. He didn't want to risk any of the other passengers being harmed.

"We would like the chest of gold, if you please. Hand it over and you good people can go away unharmed." he spoke with an air of authority, but never seemed to raise his voice. One of the men grabbed a gold necklace from Clarisse's neck, and then pried a diamond wedding ring off the Maybelle's finger, her child balled with fear.

"Hand me the money, honey." one man said to Violet as his hand reached through the window, with the other hand pointing a pistol at her head.

"No!" she screamed.

"Don't harm the passengers! All we want is the lockbox!" Their leader finally lost his patience and shouted angrily. He gave the man who had stolen the jewelry a look of disapproval.

"Come on, Snake Eyes..." he said with disappointment, and then tossed the jewelry back to the ladies.

The driver unlocked the chains which held the money box securely on top of the stagecoach. He plopped the chest down on the ground between the horses, the coins inside made musical clinking noises. Snake Eyes dragged the heavy chest back to his horse with his pistol constantly pointed at Joe. The other men slowly began to withdraw towards their leader, with their guns constantly pointed at the top of the stagecoach. Curiosity overcame her, and Violet had to look out her window to see the robber. Snake Eyes was backing up on his horse with pistol in hand. His steely green eyes stood out like emeralds on weathered skin between his hat and black bandana. Now she knew how he got his nickname. He turned his horse, and his gang followed after him on a gallop, whooping and hollering at their victory. Joe took a shot at one of the last robbers to leave but missed, they were out of range for his sawed-off shotgun.

"Dammit," the driver said in defeat, "what am I going to do when I get to Fort Concho? What am I going to tell the sergeant? You're a fool! Why didn't you shoot him, that's what they're paying you for, isn't it?"

"I couldn't shoot him!" Joe exclaimed, "He was right in the middle of horses. There was nothing I could do."

"We'll just have to report it to Wells Fargo. Dammit, I haven't had a stage robbed in the last three months!" He cursed again and snapped at the reins.

The passengers were dumbfounded, except for Jack who just went back to sleep under his hat.

Maybelle was still in shock. "He took my wedding ring my poor old Jackson gave to me… but he gave it back. Does this happen frequently?"

Doctor Colburn responded, "I believe it does ma'am. Stagecoach robberies are becoming more and more commonplace in the West."

"I'm just glad I have my ring back." Maybelle totally dismissed the near robbery of Clarisse's gold necklace, or the actual loss of the soldiers' wages.

"I don't what I'm going to tell my husband when we reach the Fort. He's been working so hard, and his troop deserved that money." Clarisse told the doctor with a sigh.

Violet wondered if the stagecoach robbers knew the money was for the soldiers in Fort Concho. The Buffalo Soldiers would have a bone to pick with them she reckoned. In fact, the entire

Union government out West might be on their trail soon enough.

She stared back out at the vast Texas plain. A head appeared in front of her, which took her out of her trance gave her a start. It was Billy. His body hung over the side of the stagecoach so he could look inside. "Everybody alright?"

Violet and the other passengers just nodded, and Billy's head disappeared.

Billy sat back up and the blood that had rushed to his head throbbed and gave him a headache. He looked around at the other passengers who chose to ride up top. There was a withered old man with a long straggly gray beard, wearing faded bib overalls. There was also a young man of what Billy guessed about fourteen years of age. He wore a very large wide-brimmed hat, which in comparison made him look even smaller. The boy had a look of frustration on his face.

"I wish I could have gotten a shot off on one of those robbers."

Billy smiled a little, he reminded him of his little brother Paul.

"Me too." Billy said, "What's your name, kid?"

"My name ain't none of your business, but people call me Jimbo."

"Well, it mightn't be none of my business, but it ain't none of yourn to travelling all the way to the likes of San Angelo unaccompanied. I reckon you stole that hat, but you didn't bother to steal a good six-shooter."

Jimbo's face went red. "I didn't have the time. See, I killed a man and had to skedaddle right quick."

"With your bare hands?" Billy said, "That must've been quite an accomplishment."

Jimbo pulled his large hat over his eyes and tried to ignore the prodding questions of Billy. He suspected Jimbo was a runaway. The dangerous encounter with the robbers made Billy appreciate the people on the stagecoach with him, and the air smelled fresh.

Violet hadn't been afraid when she screamed at the robber trying to take her money—she was just being stubborn. That was all the money she had to start a new life with Cyrus. Though she had to admit she had been afraid that Billy might try something foolish, but thank goodness that did not happen.

Her heart was still pounding wildly, but it was beginning to calm itself. Instead of beating with uncertainty about the robbers, it was fluttering in anticipation of seeing Cyrus again.

She had been told by the driver that they had one more stop before Fort Concho, and then finally San Angelo. She was nervous, excited, and mooning. There was also a pit in her stomach, but it wasn't the biscuits and gravy. She was afraid of what she might find. Would Cyrus be in good health, was he recovered? Had he changed? Would he still love her? Of course he loved her, why else would he write letters pleading for her to come to Texas and marry him? What if he had changed his mind?

What if she had changed? She went back and forth, questioning it all. It was beginning to make her head ache. She fiddled with the ring that Cyrus had given her and smiled. That simple ring represented a deep, young love. She could at least take comfort in what had happened long ago.

Violet looked out the window, there were acres of apple trees, limbs burdened with ripe red fruits. To the east she saw distant blue mountain ranges—they almost seemed like a memory compared to this flatland. Before she knew it false fronted buildings popped up on both sides.

"Alright folks. Welcome to Eden." The driver said as he opened the stagecoach door, "This is the last stop you get before Fort Concho and then San Angelo."

The doctor helped her and the other ladies out of the stagecoach. Violet surmised as to where the town got its name, the tangy, sweet smell of fresh apples floated on the wind; named for garden with the apple that tempted Eve. Eden was a small town, and the buildings looked like they had been built in hurry. Violet looked up and saw the façade of the largest building in town. It did triple duty as restaurant, hotel and saloon.

The passengers were motioned inside the building to a few large round dark wooden tables. A woman with frizzy hair and tired eyes put plates in front of each of the passengers in a hurried manner. "Special of the day…" she said.

There was pot roast, of what meat Violet didn't know, but it looked tough and stringy, possibly mule. There were green beans on the side along with a steaming square of cornbread with a pat of melting butter. Violet gobbled up the cornbread. She hadn't had homemade cornbread since she was back home in Missouri. Even though whites gave themselves credit for cornbread it was really an invention of the Indians.

Billy had not said a word to her since they had left Deer Creek before dawn. She didn't know why it bothered her so much, but it did. He sat quietly and picked at his lunch. She distracted herself by looking around the dining room. A large brass chandelier dominated the room and seemed to crowd the low ceiling. Behind the tables was a large bar, and the men there ignored the stagecoach passengers. On the brown and off-white Tudor style walls were the mounted heads of white-tail deer, mule deer, elk, and buffalo. It baffled her that white men liked to put the heads of the game they killed on walls for others to admire.

She quickly finished her food. She enjoyed the green beans in particular; she hadn't had fresh vegetables for quite some time.

The harried woman came back to collect the travelers money. Jimbo searched all of his pockets but could not come up with the silver dollar which she demanded of him. Billy reached inside his pocket and gave two of his silver dollars to the woman. She thanked Billy but eyed the fourteen year old boy with disdain.

After they were finished with their lunch, the passengers herded back out to the stagecoach. The driver was in a foul mood ever since the robbery and he just wanted to get his route over with. They pulled away with a jolt from the tiny, respectable town of Eden.

# Chapter XXIII

To the north, Violet saw a gigantic herd of buffalo. There seemed to be as many as there were stars in the night sky. Out of the corner of her eye she saw an Indian riding on horseback, and then there were two others. From their attire she thought they might be Lipan Apache, but from this distance she couldn't tell. They were armed with bows. They were hunting the buffalo, and probably did not give the stagecoach a thought. She hoped that Joe wouldn't notice the Indian hunters and fire upon them in his ignorance.

The Indian riders were closing in on a straggler on the outskirts of the enormous herd. They swooped down on the stray buffalo and the first hunter released several arrows into its thick hide and a cloud of dust billowed around as the lifeless mass fell to the ground.

The loud crack of a shotgun echoed over the plains. In the silence following the echo the ears of the buffalo twitched, and their dewy black eyes full of fear and instinct shifted. A few of the larger buffalo, the leaders, turned around restlessly. The Indians stared opened-mouthed as the buffalo herd moved like one giant organism to the south. Violet knew what was coming. Stampede.

The herd charged in one direction. They made a noise like thunder and a cloud of dust formed around them. Their massive heads pulled down to the ground, and they huffed laboriously as their spindly legs carried them faster toward the road and the stagecoach. She could hear the driver yell and curse at the horses and Joe, as he snapped the reins violently. She could see them coming, their woolly heads like battering rams. Their enormous bodies could crush a person in seconds. The herd stretched to the western horizon. Violet froze in terror, trapped inside a rattling cage. Some of the other passengers screamed. Jack pulled out his revolver ready for some hunting action. The horses, caught up in the craze of the stampede, ran like mad off the trail. The stagecoach jolted over the rough terrain, encountering more speed and obstacles that its construction should brave.

She could feel the heavy perspiration, and smells of the buffalos' breath. The noise of the stampede rang in her ears like a hundred tumbling waterfalls. The herd was almost to the stagecoach. Out of the corner of her left eye she saw a tall, scraggy tree. Billy leaped from the top of the rolling stagecoach and onto one of the branches. In seconds his hand reached out to her. He yelled at the top of his lungs, "Violet!"

She grabbed onto his forearm and she swung into his embrace. She was safe now. She watched as the stagecoach arduously made its way ahead of the stampede. Beneath her were the mad and stupefied buffalo going faster than what could be expected from their enormous size. It was a blur of brown fur and dust. She coughed the dust out from her lungs, but not without a sharp pain coming from her ribs. Billy handed her his bandana. She put it over her mouth. The buffalo just kept coming, but eventually the last few calves ran past. The stampede seemed to last for hours, though it was probably only few minutes. Violet's tired eyes could see the horizon again, finally clear of the buffalo.

To her surprise the Indian hunters were still there. They had waited for the stampede to pass. As the dust cleared around them, she could verify that they were Lipan Apache. The leader's long dark hair and hot-tempered, young, handsome face were familiar. He ran his horse to the base of the tree. As he looked up, she could tell he was White Horse. He smiled and reached his arm up to help Violet get down, and set her on his horse. Billy stood in the tree, skeptical of what White Horse would do next. White Horse reached out his hand to him too, and let Billy go on the ground.

"Thanks…" Billy said as he adjusted his hat. Violet was still on his horse, and that worried Billy. He could just run off with her, leaving him in the dust.

As White Horse stared at him he said, "A he ya eh." but Billy had no idea what that meant.

Violet said a few words to him in Apache, "Chelee?"

White Horse nodded and whistled to his party. There came one rider on a black and white pinto horse, its first half completely white except for two black feet, and the haunches and tail were jet black. He dismounted and held onto the reins.

White Horse yelled and ran off to the northwest with Violet. Billy stood there stunned for a moment and then grabbed the reins from the Apache and jumped onto the pinto and took chase. He cursed under his breath.

The breeze swept through her hair, and White Horse gave her a playful grin as they rode up a small hill. She had no idea what was going on, but it certainly wasn't a kidnapping. She trusted White Horse enough to know that she would be safe, especially since she had saved his life once. They stopped on top of a hill. He took her off his horse gently, and turned to face her. He was tall, at least six feet and had the rangy build of a plains warrior.

"I never thought I would see you again, nah-lin." He brushed away a lock of hair from her face. "I believe the Great Spirit brought you here." His once playful face turned serious, and he put his hands gently on her arms.

Violet's heart thumped faster, she knew what was coming.

"Shil nzoo." White Horse said.

She couldn't remember what it meant, because she had never heard it spoken before. Her eyes widened in confusion.

White Horse's eyebrows lowered in exasperation, "I love you."

Her eyes grew even wider. She was speechless; there were no words in English or Apache to explain to him her predicament.

"White Horse... Ashoge. You are a brave warrior and a good man," He began to smile in hope of her loving him too. "But... I have promised my love to someone else."

His dark eyes filled with sadness. "Hat'ugha?" White Horse gestured his head questioningly toward Billy, coming up the trail.

Violet shook her head. "Not him. I'm sorry."

White Horse bit his lower lip in bitter disappointment and embarrassment.

"I would be a terrible wife for you. I have no idea how to tan buffalo hides—I can barely cook.

You need a woman who can give you lots of children, and be the wife of a great Chief. I would want to ride horses all day. I'm no good for you. You will find a good woman—an Apache woman—trust me."

"But I want *you*, Violet." White Horse desperately pleaded, "We can ride together. You would be free to do what you want."

He leaned in for a kiss. Violet pulled her head back and shook her head again.

"I'm sorry, White Horse. We are from different worlds. You would regret marrying me." She hugged White Horse and whispered in his ear, "Gunjule, shils aash... Egogahan." Then she kissed him on the cheek. His sad eyes were understanding of her reasons, yet still full of heartbreak.

She turned around and there was Billy, twenty feet away, sitting with his arms crossed, resting them on the saddle horn. White Horse quickly mounted his steed and flew off in the opposite direction.

"It's not what you think." Violet said as she blushed.

"No. I get it, birds of a feather."

Her fists clenched and her face grew even redder with anger.

"It's not what you think. White Horse is a good man." she said in exasperation, "Let's get out of here. By the way we can keep the horse." She pushed Billy to the back and climbed into the saddle.

"Now I know what took you so long in the tipi—" he began.

She interrupted him with a finger pointed up to the sky, "If you say one more word Billy Colton, I will kick you off this horse—so help me God." She kicked the horse and off they went riding in the last direction of the stagecoach.

# Chapter XXIV

Violet wished that her last meeting with White Horse might have gone smoother. She had managed to break not one young man's heart, but two. Her stomach churned with the thought of it. She never had the best rapport with men. They were always more sensitive than they let on, and she could be so abrasive. She felt terrible. She was a heartbreaker and she hadn't intended to be.

They kept riding until the bright red stagecoach was spotted. It was toppled over, and the yellow wheels were still slowly spinning. Unhitched, the horses walked about nervously. The driver stood over the wooden heap, exasperated. Joe was still there, but had backed several feet away from the driver, as if he were a keg of dynamite about to blow. The other passengers were standing about the stagecoach in a stupor. The doctor tended to the slightly bumped, bruised, and injured. The driver noticed Billy and Violet for the first time since their leap from the stagecoach, his face as white as a ghost's.

"What happened to y'all? Tarnation! We thought you was thrown out—y'all plum disappeared!"

"I took the liberty to grab onto a passing tree." Billy said.

"Oh," Was all the driver could muster as he stared at the pair and their newly acquired pinto in disbelief. "Where did you get the horse?" The driver demanded with a pointed finger at the pony.

"It's a long story." Violet said with a clenched jaw.

This time the driver only nodded in response, though still confused at their new acquisition.

Maybelle sat on the ground with her child in her lap. She glared at Clarisse as if she had summoned the buffalo stampede with some unknown dark powers. Clarisse nursed a bruised arm as she waited for the doctor to finish tending to the withered old man.

"I'm so glad y'all two are alive!" She said as she lifted her eyes up to Violet and Billy.

"Thank you Clarisse." Violet paused for a second trying to find something appropriate to say to the other passengers, "We weren't sure what happened to the stage. Glad to see everyone is safe."

Billy alighted the horse and searched the area. He knew that his saddlebags had to be around the stagecoach somewhere. Scattered passengers' luggage was everywhere in heaps of leather and carpet. Some of the doctor's bottles of precious medicine had been shattered and the fluid dripped out onto the dry ground, already beginning to evaporate in the hot sun. Billy searched through the debris for his dilapidated saddlebags. He found them, the leather had been crushed and his saddlebags were covered in a layer of dust, almost unrecognizable.

Violet hopped off the horse to search for her belongings. Her saddlebags they were in slightly better shape than Billy's, having dodged most of the stampede being strapped to the top of the stagecoach. She saw a white piece of paper lying next to the indentation in the dust left from Billy's saddlebag. She stooped down and picked it up, and slipped it into her dress skirt pocket for safekeeping.

"Is everybody alright?" Billy asked Dr. Colburn.

"Everyone checks out fine. We can get this show on the road, as soon as you're ready sir." he said as he looked at the driver.

"As long as we can get this hunk of wood right-side-up... Alright boys, let's get a move on!" The driver said as he rolled up his sleeves on his brawny, hairy arms. The healthy men of the party (including the young boy, Jimbo) placed their fingers under the gigantic wooden structure and lifted. With hard work, grunts and sweat the stagecoach was righted. Amazingly enough, the superstructure remained intact, and the wheels were unbroken and ready to roll.

The driver clapped his dusty hands together and resulted in a raucous echo, "Let's move on outta here folks. Just hop right back in there... might be a little dusty, but don't mind that."

Violet stepped toward the stagecoach door, but then remembered the little black and white pinto that had been so generously donated by White Horse's tribe. She might need a horse. She looked back at Billy, already he had put his saddlebags on it.

"If you don't mind me I'll be tagging along with the pony, hate to leave it out here." he said to the driver.

"Alright, but I expect at least half of your fare fee."

Billy nodded and mounted the horse and rode up next to Violet, "You can ride in the stage, me and the pony'll do just fine. Couldn't carry two people for too long anyhow."

"Alright, but I get to keep him when we're done." Violet said with a teasing, pert smile, "he was intended for me anyway."

Soon they were on their way again. The ride was not as smooth as before the buffalo stampede.

The whole capsule seemed to tilt to the left, which gave Violet an uneasy feeling. There were also the occasional creaks and squeaks interrupting the passenger's conversation or sleeping plans.

The stampede had been exciting, and had given Violet some added adrenaline. It made her realize that she couldn't predict what life would throw at her, but she could survive. She had survived this entire journey with lasting toughness, and she was almost finished. How great would be her joy when she would be able to see Cyrus's face again!

She fiddled with the fabric on her skirt, anxiously trying to find something to do with her empty hands. She was even more excited to arrive in San Angelo, worry and fear had gone out the window for her. Fire began to rise up within her heart. Whatever ahead lay ahead and she welcomed it with intense vivacity and fervor. The world was full of brilliant possibilities.

Her fingers ran across the wrinkled letter in her pocket. She had almost forgotten it was there, and might have completely forgotten it if she hadn't been fidgeting so much. This was the same letter she had discovered days earlier in Billy's saddlebag, but she never opened it. She softly pulled it out and unfolded the page. She was hesitant and cautious, as if Billy were looking over her shoulder. Good thing there weren't windows in the back of the stagecoach. Eventually curiosity got the better of her, and she began to read. The script was written in long, sharp letters.

Dear Mr. Colton,

It has come to my attention that your property of approximately 10,000 acres would be a desirable addition to my current landholdings. It would be of great use to me in my business enterprises. I would be willing to offer ten percent more than its current value, on the condition that the property would be sold in its entirety. Otherwise, we may have to send negotiators to convince you of the sale.

Undersigned,

Mr. James Smith

Violet gasped when she read the undersigned. She recalled back to the moment in the cave when Billy had mentioned his name before. Was this the same James Smith, brother of the hated Jasper? There was something very unsettling about the letter, particularly the word *negotiators*. Billy was in more trouble than he had let on. She knew that the reach of the Smith brothers was far, but how far? Could their money, power, friends and influence reach all the way to San Angelo? A chill ran down her spine and she quickly folded the letter back up and shoved it back in her pocket.

# Chapter XXV

The prairie seemed endless in Violet's eyes. The farther they traveled west it became drier, almost desert-like. It was so much different than her home in Missouri, so densely wooded and one could scarcely find a plot of flat land to farm or to build a house upon. It was the exact opposite of her peoples', the Cherokee homeland. The hills and pines of Georgia were ancient, wild and dignified. They were green, and abundant in numerous forms of life. The prairie was ancient as well, the smell of earth and sod and the existence of the buffalo all attested to that. Certainly there was life, but it was much different. There was a certain strangeness that emanated from loneliness and desolation that was impossible to ignore.

Dust appeared from a large troop of riders on the right. They were much unlike the bandits she had witnessed earlier in the day. They were well organized, and the entire troop was made up of black men.

Violet was excited to see those whom she had only heard of before. They were carried by a rag-tag group of brown horses, of different sizes and shapes. The horses were well cared for, but many were old and sickly and not fit to ride the frontier. The men were clad with the dark blue uniforms of the Union, which had been so hated by Southerners just four short years before, but were now a staple in the West and a symbol of the United States' power in the region, especially over the Indians. The unnatural dark blue coats and sky blue pants with the bright yellow stripe on the side stood in sharp contrast to the dry and dusty earth-toned surroundings.

The soldier leading them was wearing a dark blue cavalry cap with the recognizable crossed sabers. He was in his early thirties. His face was serious, with clear brown eyes and intense, heavy-set eyebrows, as if his responsibilities rested above them. The square shape of his jaw was accentuated by a closely-trimmed black beard. It was a proud and handsome face. On his jacket sleeve were three yellow chevrons, which indicated that he was a sergeant.

"Howdy," Violet could hear the driver say with a quavering voice.

"Good day," the sergeant said, "we have been instructed to escort this stagecoach and its passengers to Fort Concho due to the increases of hostile Indian attacks." He spoke everything with steady authority.

"Thank you... Uh, there's something I have to tell you sarge. We lost the lockbox about fifteen miles or so ago."

The sergeant's eyes widened and showed the bright whites of his eyes, but then he relaxed again.

"You said fifteen miles ago? What did these bandits look like?" His strong voice began to waver.

"Yes, sir. I can't rightly recollect since they was disguised. They had rags on their faces."

"I see. Which direction were they headed?"

"Due west."

"And you were unable to stop them?" the sergeant questioned and glanced at Joe, with the shotgun still in his lap. The young shotgunner had a look of sour disgust and disappointment.

Joe spoke up, still with a steeply pointed frown on his face, "No, sir. I could not. He mixed himself up with the horses, and I couldn't risk shooting, and maybe killing some of them—then we'd be stuck for good…"

"I see, thank you for the information gentlemen. I will proceed with my original orders. Move out!" He raised his yellow-gloved hand, whistled and the Ninth Cavalry moved west toward Fort Concho. Clarisse had her neck craned at a most uncomfortable angle to watch the cavalry troop.

"That was my husband." she said with a mixture of pride and relief, she smiled knowing that he was still safe, but that happy look soon turned to worry over his lost wages.

"Who?" Violet asked.

"The sergeant."

After about an hour of riding—which seemed like an eternity—something appeared on the flat, empty prairie horizon. There were several buildings built from limestone rock. They looked like large houses, complete with square white columns, and dark green shutters on the windows. Some of the buildings were connected with boardwalks to protect the soldier's boots from the often muddy grounds.

The fort was large, and the buildings were formed in a rectangle, and open to the prairie. It was situated at the fork in the Concho River, and with water being so scarce around these parts it was quite a practical location. As Violet looked around she noticed that some buildings were still being constructed by the troops. It was still new, and it looked as though it had been built hastily to supply the growing population of San Angelo and the surrounding area with protection from the Comanche. The troop preceded them, and directed the stagecoach in front of the flag pole in the middle of the parade, to a small wooden office building to their right. As they were about to get out to stretch their legs, Maybelle refused to budge, even though the doctor offered to help her out. "I'm fine. I ain't going out there." she said stubbornly with her arms crossed.

Violet rolled her eyes, stepped out and breathed in the fresh air. There was the smell of newly moved earth, mineral smells from the limestone, and earthy horse smells from the stables. Billy dismounted the black and white pinto and stretched his long legs.

"So this is what a fort looks like? Well I'll be..." Billy said with eyes wide-open with wonder.

Clarisse was helped out of the stagecoach, and was about ready to rush over to her husband, but she stopped herself.

Sergeant Hopkins was speaking earnestly with the driver. Clarisse's eyes saddened. She had so hoped to spend time with her husband, but now she knew that finding the robbers would occupy much of his time.

"It'll be alright," Violet sympathized, "I'm sure they'll catch the bandits soon."

The driver was red with shame and frustration. Joe was white-faced and knew what was coming.

"Once we get back to Austin, you're fired!" The driver calmed himself and addressed the passengers, "They'll be sending the word out to the local sheriff. He talked of a reward, but he's not sure when it'll be implemented."

Jack had lit up one of his cigars, puffing away and immune to the conversation, until his eyebrows perked up with the word reward. Clarisse was escorted to her husband's quarters adjoining one of the barracks, not by her husband but one of the lower-ranking officers. Her head hung low on her dignified frame. Violet saw in the corner of her eye that Clarisse reached the doorway, and the other officer left. Sergeant Hopkins walked up to her by surprise, took off his hat and solidly embraced his wife. Violet smiled. Billy blushed as he turned on his heel away from Violet.

"Alright folks, let's get a move-on. Hopefully we don't drive into a crack and down to hell." The driver said woefully. Sergeant Hopkins returned from saying hello and goodbye to his wife and led the Buffalo Soldiers to escort the stagecoach to San Angelo.

# Chapter XXVI

San Angelo was located just a few miles south of the fort, across the Concho River. Violet began to see signs of non-militarized civilization, which excited her. As long as the wheels of the stagecoach kept spinning, she would see Cyrus very soon. The air changed suddenly, and the scattered grey clouds which had been looming overhead earlier clumped together. It began to rain. She stuck her hand out the window to feel the precious drops of life on her skin. She felt like her entire time in Texas had been parched of water. This was a good omen.

She looked out the window and saw hundreds of Longhorn cattle quietly enduring the rain. They had the longest horns she had ever seen. One particular mottled brown old steer had at least a seven foot span. She knew this was why Cyrus was down here. These half-wild cows gave him a living.

She brought her hand back inside the stagecoach and dried it on her skirt. She untied the knot of the silky, yellow ribbon which kept the stack of letters from Cyrus together. She pulled one out for directions, it read. "I am currently residing at the DeWitt Hotel. It is one of the largest buildings in town and next to Veck's General Store and Saloon…" She closed the letter. She was beginning to grow nervous. She had imagined meeting him several times in her imagination. But what if he was still ill, or even worse? Her hands trembled. What if she couldn't find him at the hotel? The doctor had been killed. She knew nothing else. All the information that she had to go on for this entire journey was wrapped up in that yellow ribbon. She would find out what she needed to know, her ingenuity hadn't failed her yet.

She looked outside. A town had sprung out of nothing. There were several dilapidated canvas tents left over from the civil war on the outskirts of town. If there were wooden or limestone buildings, most were unfinished, and several had huge pieces of canvas covering the bare skeletons of their wooden frames. The dirt roads were freshly covered in mud from the rain, which was still pouring on the West Texas town. But the residents were still out in force. There were ladies dressed in finery she had never seen before, but it was a shabby kind of finery, as if a pigeon were trying to be a dove. There were a few wealthy men, dressed in their finest duds of silk top hats and wool suits. There were a few colorful looking ones with wide panama hats and bowlers that she thought must be gamblers. She could hear tinny piano music coming from virtually every building. Men walked out of these buildings swaying, and crookedly walked onto the street, some with liquor bottles still in hand. She despised alcohol, and the sight of the men going to and coming from the plentiful saloons made her sick. She peeked into one of these make-shift buildings and saw the player piano, the bar that served only whiskey, the buxom ladies-of-the-night, and drunken cowboys. She turned her head away in disgust. This is the town in which Cyrus was living? Well, he was living here because he was a cowboy. Surely he had more morality than those occupying the saloons.

The stagecoach pulled up to Veck's General Store and Saloon. The building was split evenly between the two by a painted white line. On one side was the bar, which was quieter than the fifteen others in the town. On the other side was the general store with a smiling clerk with a waxed-up handle-bar mustache behind the counter. The darkness and the rain subsided quickly, but the light grey clouds still hung overhead. Billy tied the pony to the hitching post and went to Violet's side. He knew that she was vulnerable in this town, and needed his protection, even if she wouldn't acknowledge it herself. She had almost forgotten that Billy was still with her in the excitement of possibly meeting Cyrus in San Angelo.

"Final stop, folks." The remaining passengers began to pile out, Jack, Doctor Colburn and Maybelle Hawthorne. The driver curled his fingers toward him gesturing for the payment from the passengers, Billy parted with his payment for half-fare. Violet pulled out the money from her leather pouch. She had finally arrived.

Jack had that knowing smile on his face and walked up to Violet, close enough for a whisper. Violet felt uncomfortable being this close to him.

"I've come to apologize for my behavior in the stagecoach. I know your secret. You can try to hide it, but I can see it." He then whispered in her ear, "I've seen plenty of half-breeds in my time." Jack walked away with a wave, "Good luck miss."

The doctor walked up to her and shook her hand and wished her good luck. "I hope we'll be able to meet again, young lady." He smiled.

"I hope so too, doctor. Where is your practice?"

"It's just over yonder." He motioned to a short building which had the word Apothecary painted across the top of the façade. Just then Violet remembered something, "Excuse me, Doctor Colburn. Do you know who was the previous... operator?"

"If I recall correctly, his name was Dr. Furstenberg. May I ask why?"

"I knew a patient of his." Violet said shyly.

"I see. Good day now." he said before he crossed the busy street to the apothecary.

"Good luck in San Angelo!" The driver said in haste as he snapped at the reins after he collected all the money from the passengers. The stagecoach drove away, flinging mud in every direction. Almost every inch of her skirt was covered in it. She stared down at it in disappointment. She began to panic. She didn't want Cyrus to see her for the first time in years looking like she had rolled around in a pig sty. Her eyes hurriedly looked around for some sort of clothing shop. At the end of street was a shop that looked somewhat respectable, where men's and ladies clothing were displayed in the large window. She stamped along the muddy road to the clothing shop. Billy followed after her. Inside the shop she noticed some very fine expensive clothing, much more expensive than what she had seen back home. She supposed it was because they were so far out west, and expensive material was hard to come by. There were many ornately decorated dresses, some with hoopskirts, and some with the slimmer bustled styles.

There was one that caught her eye. It had a jade green taffeta bodice, and a white skirt trimmed with lace and green ribbon, complete with a taffeta bustle. The green in it reminded her of Cyrus's eyes. She had come all this way, and she thought she might as well look pretty. She took it off the mannequin. She stopped and asked the store clerk if she could try it on.

She was shown to a small closet. She struggled with the stay, due to her injured ribs. She did not lace it tightly and only wore it for convention. It fit her beautifully. The dress highlighted her complexion and made her dark eyes stand out. She walked out and picked up the rest of the ensemble, the white bonnet with green ribbon, and the green taffeta parasol. She didn't care if it cost a fortune—she just wanted to look nice for Cyrus, she wanted to be as beautiful as he remembered her being so many years ago.

She stepped out of the shop. Billy was standing in the street. Still curious as to why Violet had entered the dress shop. His mouth hung open. He had never seen Violet look so lady-like. She swayed with joy, and the skirt swayed with her. Billy had always known that Violet was beautiful, she didn't have to put on a fancy dress and duds to prove it. She glowing in anticipation to see Cyrus again. Part of Billy wished that that glow was for him, but he smiled anyway because she was happy.

Billy put his arm out for her, but he knew that she should be escorted, especially since she was dressed like that. She lifted her skirts, careful not to get mud on the snowy-white ruffled hem, and took Billy's arm carefully with a charming smile.

The DeWitt hotel was only a few buildings down the road. Violet's heart began to flutter as the moment of truth came closer. She walked into the shabby looking large hotel. She wriggled her arm away from Billy and gently motioned him to sit in the chair in the lobby, he reluctantly obeyed. He stepped aside because he knew this was her moment. She had been waiting for this since she left Missouri.

She walked up to the counter to ask the critical question, "Does Cyrus Morgan have a room here?" she asked uneasily, nervous of the outcome.

The lackadaisical desk clerk responded, "He sure does, but he's not in right now missy. Can I take a message?"

Violet gasped audibly upon hearing the news. Her heart began to pound violently, and visible weight had been lifted off her shoulders, hearing that he was still alive. "Do you know where he could possibly be?" she asked pleadingly.

"Sure do, might be in the Lone Star Saloon."

"Where is that exactly?"

"It's around the corner, past Miss Hattie's Place."

"Thank you, sir." Violet said as she hurried out the hotel door.

"Where are you going?" Billy asked, surprised at her leaving so soon.

"The Lone Star Saloon," she responded. He ran to catch up with her in the muddy street. She trudged onward, picking her skirt up past her ankles to avoid the mud. Billy knew not to leave Violet alone, especially with her dressed like this. He could already tell that she was garnering a lot of unwanted attention by the wolf whistles from the drunken men on the street. He stuck close by her with his eyes darting around and his hand conscious of the revolver at his side. Finally they made it to the Lone Star Saloon. It was another one of those half-finished buildings with large pieces of canvas acting as the entrance. There was a warm glow of lamplight, and the sound of piano and conversation came from inside. Violet lifted the canvas over her head and stepped in fearlessly. The voices went silent, and even the piano music stopped as the piano player turned around and all the occupants stared slack-jawed at the well-dressed lady who just entered. Violet had forgotten for a moment that she was wearing fine ladies clothing and not dressed like a man. This was going to be tricky. She scanned the room, seeing no one at first that looked like her handsome Cyrus. Sadness struck her and she turned around to leave when a tall well-framed man stood up from a poker table.

"Violet, is that you?" came the slow question from a gentlemanly southern accent. He threw off his hat, revealing his jet black hair that grew silver near his temples, although he was still a young man. His teeth gleamed pearly white as a smile beamed from his tanned face. His mustache had grown wild and long almost reaching his chin, stubble covered the rest of his jaw. His eyes were like bright shining emeralds against leather. For a moment, Violet didn't recognize him. His demeanor had changed. His voice and his skin were rough, hardened by life on the frontier. But it was him, it was Cyrus.

Violet smiled the broadest smile possible. "Cyrus!"

"Violet, you look prettier than a magnolia blossom!" Cyrus laughed as he took her in his arms and swung her around. Violet winced with pain when he set her down. "Oh, are you alright? What's happened?"

"I-I'm fine. I received a little injury that's all."

"I'm sorry my love. It's so good to see you!" he said as he put his hardened hands on her warm face. The crowd in the saloon began to speak in hushed murmured tones, still disenfranchised that a respectable lady had entered the saloon. Cyrus, seeing the commotion took Violet's hand.

"Come on. Let's go."

Billy had all but disappeared. For a split second Violet wondered where he might be, but then she looked back at Cyrus and forgot about it.

It started raining again. She opened her parasol and the reunited lovers ran onto the DeWitt hotel's small covered porch seeking shelter from the downpour.

"I almost can't believe you're here. I thought you might have—" Violet began breathlessly, but Cyrus put his fingertips on her lips to stop her.

"Don't talk of that. I'm fine. I'm so glad *you're* here." They both smiled and looked into each other's eyes. "There are so many things I want to tell you Violet, but—" The spark left his green eyes and his once joyous expression turned somber as his eyebrows tightened together, creating fine lines on his forehead.

"What is it?" She questioned concernedly.

"It's nothing dearest," he said in his upper-class southern tone, relaxing again, "you're even more beautiful than I remembered." Cyrus brushed away a stray wet lock of her hair away from her eyes. She grinned and almost giggled with happiness.

"I missed you." she said. Though his appearance was rougher and he was older, he was still the handsome boy that she had met many years ago, and had loved. Those eyes were still as green as oak leaves in the spring. She could feel the warmth of his body as he leaned in closer to her. The spark in his emerald eyes turned to fire. He kissed a passion to make up for the lost years. She moved in closer as her hand passed from his sinewy shoulder to the nape of his neck. She could smell the warm scent of prairie musk. His lips were rough, but still soft against hers and full of life, but there was something hard and cold in that kiss. Different from the shy ones they had shared years before, something almost menacing.

They were interrupted by a voice in the street, "Hey Cyrus!" the voice called out, "it's your play in the game! Or are you going to lose all that money?"

Cyrus looked at the man in the street regretfully.

"I'll be back. Stay where you are." he said with a cheeky grin.

Violet stood alone on the porch. She was partially giddy with happiness, and part discomfited. This was not how she had expected it to go. But that didn't matter. She was in San Angelo and Cyrus was here, and still alive! He had kissed her and said all the things she had longed to hear. Everything would work out, she reassured herself. She opened the door to the hotel and stepped inside from the pouring rain.

The sleazy hotel clerk had seen the kiss because he had a bawdy smile on his face.

"So, do you kiss every strange man you come across?" he said.

Violet was taken aback and replied with disgust, "That is none of your business sir. And that strange man happens to be my fiancé… and he's a very good shot." she said as she glared over the counter at him. The desk clerk stopped smiling and stared at her wide-eyed. "I'll have a room please."

The clerk shakily placed a key on the desk and she made her way up to her room.

She tossed the parasol on the unsound bed, and took off her bonnet. She smiled as she laid down. She was exhausted, body and soul. Her entire body was warm with the knowledge that Cyrus was still alive, and apparently still loved her.

# Chapter XXVII

Violet rubbed the sand out of her eyes after she awoke. The night before, slumber overtook her akin to a being wrapped in a warm blanket. The combined fatigue from her journey to San Angelo settled in on her body once she had had a chance to rest. Added to this was the grand emotional rapture triggered by the discovery that Cyrus was alive and well. These effects combined together made her sink into a state of delicious exhaustion.

The sunlight streamed through her window. Violet opened it, and a cool breeze that seemed to beckon in the fall blew into her room. That summer had been so long and hot in Texas that she thought it might remain hot forever. The meadowlarks outside her window were chirping sweetly.

As her eyes adjusted to the sunlight, she wondered where Cyrus might be now. Her thoughts wandered to Billy. She hadn't seen him since she met Cyrus at the Lone Star Saloon, and wondered where her faithful companion might be now. It seemed strange now that he had disappeared without saying so much as a word to Cyrus.

A pang of mysterious emptiness filled her heart. Could Billy have left her in San Angelo now that his task was finished? He had responsibilities, family, and friends back home in Mustang Ridge. Perhaps he left to go back to them. Maybe she hadn't meant as much to him as she had suspected. This selfishly made her sad, if it were the case. Although she couldn't, shouldn't be sad now that she had Cyrus. She had so much to tell him.

She dressed quickly, rearranged her hair, washed her face, and pinched her cheeks to bring them some of the rosy color that was expected of girls. She put on her bonnet and set off to find Cyrus. Perhaps he was breakfasting, she thought. She walked down the creaky stairs of the hotel. Silently she thanked God that the desk clerk was absent. She opened the guestbook to find Cyrus's name and room number. She found his elegant signature a few pages back. Pleasantly, she discovered he was in the room across the hall from her. She walked back up the stairs and knocked on his door, hoping she would find him there. She waited for a response, but none came. The door was cracked slightly open so she pushed it open. No one was home. She let herself in for a moment. His hat was gone. The bed was made. He was definitely out. She closed the door softly behind her, and went spritely back down the stairs. As she walked out of the DeWitt Hotel she was shocked to see Billy on the black and white pony in the middle of the street.

"Billy!" she burst out, a little too joyously.

"Howdy Violet," he said formally with a tip of his hat.

"I-I wasn't sure that you were still in town."

"I came to return your horse." he said. He sat up stiffly on the saddle. In the excitement of the last few days, Violet had almost forgotten that she owned a horse.

"What are your plans?" she asked, her eyes moving from him to the ground.

"Well, I ain't got no more than a few pennies to my name. I reckon to find a job. Can't make the journey back like this..." he said spreading his arms out to point out his abject poverty.

She nodded. A pit grew in her stomach. She felt like she should say something to him. She hadn't even bothered to say thank you for all that he had done for her. She walked up to the horse, and patted it on the neck. She looked up at Billy. His expression was different than usual, his brow was deeply furrowed and his expression was serious. The normal winsome glow in his eyes did not shine.

"You didn't have to do anything for me. I was a total stranger to you before." she began, "Thank you, for all that you have done, all that you have sacrificed..." she trailed off, unsure of how to express her feelings of gratitude.

"I'd be happy to do it again ma'am." he said with deep sincerity.

"I wish there was something I could do for you in return... Keep the horse, Billy."

"Aw shucks, I can't take it from you."

"I want you to have it."

"Thank you, ma'am, I reckon I ain't got no other choice if you've got yer mind made up." His face turned serious. "I hope you'll be happy with Cyrus. I won't be seeing you around since you'll be a married woman soon. Goodbye Violet." He tipped his hat politely. He held her gaze with those blue eyes, within those eyes was something desperate, but it was held back by the reins of honor. For a moment the normal charming sparkle flickered across them and then faded. He rode down the street, away from her.

The pit in her stomach returned. She could hardly believe what had just happened. She could tell by his face and his expression that he still had feelings for her. She turned pale at the thought of it. She reached out for the column of hotel porch for strength. That was it. Billy was gone and she would marry Cyrus, just like she promised many years ago. For the first time in her life she was unsure if she was ready to marry him. Since the

War, she hardly knew the man he had become. His face and arms and lips were familiar, but she didn't know anything about him except from what she knew as a child, and the letters that he had sent her from the Confederate rifle pits. Her face and her palms began to sweat as she came to full realization of her situation. Did she really want to marry Cyrus? Of course she did, she said to herself reassuringly. She loved Cyrus.

Did she really love Cyrus? This question struck her as if she had betrayed her own heart and soul. How could she think such things? She wiped the nervous sweat away from her brow, she was overthinking everything. If she could find Cyrus and talk to him everything would be better.

She hurriedly walked to the nearest restaurant, as she stifled back tears, to try to find Cyrus. She opened up the batwing doors. The smell of fresh hoecakes wafted through the air. She scanned the room and there was Cyrus, sitting alone at a table eating a breakfast of hoecakes dripping with butter and molasses. Once he saw her he pulled out a chair for her and invited her to join him.

"I didn't know where you were staying," Cyrus said, "Otherwise I would have invited you to breakfast."

"I'm at the DeWitt hotel." Violet replied.

"Same as I!" He noticed her frazzled expression. "What's wrong?"

She smiled weakly, "It's nothing." and took Cyrus's hand from across the table. The touch of his hand was reassuring and seemed to curb the ebb and flow of her confusion. His eyes widened as he noticed the make-shift engagement ring made out of a horseshoe nail on her finger.

"I almost can't believe you still have it..." he said.

"What? Did you think I'd throw it away?" Violet was indignant.

"No, it's just old memories..." he said with an amused smile, "I've got enough money now to buy you a pretty engagement ring, one with a real diamond."

Violet smiled because she appreciated the gesture, "I like the old one just fine."

"I'll buy you the finest ring west of Europe. There's no need for you to keep that piece of scrap metal."

Violet frowned. She loved that ring for its simplicity and that it symbolized young love. Every time she looked at it she thought of Cyrus, it had given her strength on her long journey. She would always treasure that ring, and even if it were replaced with the finest diamonds in the world she would always keep that little piece of iron close to her heart.

"If you wish to buy me a wedding ring, that's fine. But I want to keep this piece of scrap metal." She stared at him intently as she spoke the last two words.

"Alright, keep it as long as you wish." He patted her hand somewhat condescendingly, like a parent consoling a child. He swallowed down the last bite of hoecake with a swig of hot coffee.

"What did you do last night?" Violet asked the seemingly innocent question.

Cyrus was taken aback by this, but quickly recovered to his natural suavity.

"Just played a few hands of poker with my friends."

"When can I meet them?" Violet asked, eager to get to know Cyrus's life better.

"I'm not sure they're the type of company you would like to spend time with."

"Oh?"

"They're crude men Violet, you wouldn't like them."

"I think I'll be the judge of that when I meet them." she said coolly as she took a sip of the steaming hot coffee the waitress had set in front of her. "Cyrus, I haven't spoken to you in so long. I want to hear everything about the war and—"

He interrupted her harshly, "No talk of that."

Violet blinked, as she looked at him in surprise. She had never been yelled at by Cyrus before.

"I'm—I'm sorry. I didn't know…" she said, still in shock.

"I'm sorry too dearest. I prefer never for you to speak of it again."

She was perplexed. She had never been banned from speaking on a certain subject; one of the things that Cyrus loved about her when they were young was her willingness to speak her mind.

She then realized that the war must have been a terrible experience for him, something to be hidden away forever and never to be spoken of again. She had to be more sensitive with him—it was like walking on eggshells.

She tried to change the subject, "What are your plans for today?"

"Well, the season is over, there's not much to do around here in general."

"You could show me around town." she suggested.

"Violet," he said with a frustrated sigh, "San Angelo isn't anything to see, especially compared with back home."

A grey glaze went over his eyes. Violet recalled the frightening day that the Yankees rode in. She remembered the fire. The fire that colored the sky red for hours. The Yankees had skipped past her family's humble cabin, being secluded in the woods and far enough from the main road to be of little consequence. They made Cyrus's home the target of their greed and bloodlust. The Morgan plantation was a prime example of everything the Yankees hated most about the South. Just two weeks earlier Mrs. Morgan received news that her husband had died of a gangrene infection in his legs in South Carolina. When the Union Army rode up to her doorstep she and her three daughters were all dressed in black crepe. She herself wore a black veil down to her ankles. Her youngest son, Darius, hid behind his mother while the Yankee troops invaded their home. He was only eight years old, but tall for his age. He pulled out a small wooden pistol. An officer, shaken from recent battle and prone to shoot at anything that moved discharged his weapon. The little boy died almost instantly. The commanding officer panicked, he ordered his men to empty the food from the pantry, to take any other supplies, and valuables. Darius's mother knelt there with the child in her arms. No tears issued from her eyes, but her cry was terrible, just a deep penetrating sob. Once the Yankees had plundered all they could they barricaded the doors. The commanding officer issued the order to burn it, afraid of the consequences that might be had if they knew that one of his company had shot and killed a little boy. The sisters banged on the doors as the torches were thrown through the windows. The smoke overwhelmed the girls and the mother was overcome by grief. None of them survived. She recalled the painful memory of writing Cyrus with the devastating and unspeakable news.

Violet strained to change the subject again to something a little more hopeful, "What about the ranch you told me about? I can't wait to see it."

"You'll see it, all in good time my dear." He patted her hand again, but this time she drew it back.

He got up suddenly out of his chair and put his hat on. He had a mischievous smirk on his face.

"I'm going to take you shopping." he said.

Violet got up obediently and followed him out of the restaurant. They walked down the wooden boardwalks that connected the lonely buildings. Her ears perked up as she heard the steady clip-clop of horse hooves behind her. Ever since her journey her senses were heightened and she was alert to any changes around her. She turned her head, and she saw a large silvery-white Arabian horse. The rider wore a wide flat-brimmed black hat, and a white voluminous fur coat, even though it wasn't quite chilly enough for it yet. There were two pistols situated cross-draw tucked into his shining silver belt and holsters. He carried himself with an indignant air of self-importance.

Violet whispered to Cyrus, "Who's that?"

"Never mind that," His green eyes were shaky and nervous. He waited for him to ride down the length of the street before he answered her question. "Edmund Forrester, he's what you would call a bad man."

"You mean a hired gun?" Violet whispered, trying to keep a low-profile. She had experience with hired guns unbeknownst to him.

He nodded, "That's right. He's an Englishman with a foul temper. I am unaware to what he's doing in town. He only travels somewhere if he has some *business* to settle, I heard that he was up in Montana last." Cyrus watched the rider intently until he hitched up at the post. "Come on." He grabbed Violet's hand and led her hurriedly into a small shop.

Violet thought that Cyrus was acting rather strange. He had no reason to be nervous around a hired gun.

Her eyes widened as she realized that Billy was still a wanted man. Perhaps that was the *business* that Edmund Forrester was supposed to take care of. She began to feel nauseated. No, he couldn't be in town to kill Billy. Could the Smith brothers influence reach all the way to San Angelo? Then she recalled the letter that she had read yesterday in the stagecoach. The Smiths had even more reason to have Billy killed than simple public humiliation. If they killed him, James would have even more leverage to procure the Colton's ranch. Hank Colton would have no choice but to relinquish his property or see the rest of his family suffer in a full-out range war. She had to find Billy and warn him.

"We're here now." Cyrus said. She was knocked out of her head full of terrible thoughts and back to reality.

"Where?" she asked, her face was pallid.

"In the jewelry shop you silly goose." Cyrus teased her and he pinched her cheek.

"Oh." she said as she looked down at the glass case full of rings, necklaces, brooches and bracelets. They were all different in style and craftsmanship, jewels, material and size. It looked as though poor settlers had sold their jewelry from Europe and back East; perhaps some were stolen by desperadoes and then pawned. She recalled that day when the stagecoach was robbed and their jewelry was almost taken, it might have ended up here. These thoughts made her sad, the sparkle in the jewels didn't even catch her eye and seemed dull to her.

"I don't know if I can look right now..." she said.

"What's wrong? I have the means..." Cyrus said.

"I don't know," she said, "maybe it's too soon."

Cyrus green eyes softened with disappointment, "I suppose that's alright. If you see something that catches your eye, just inform me. I'll be over there." His boots clunked as he walked over to the fancy suits, hats, and duds for men.

She gave looking for a ring another shot, she brought her head closer to the glass case to inspect them, but even the emeralds and the diamonds couldn't distract her from the inherent danger that Billy might be in.

She walked up to Cyrus. "I can't find anything right now that catches my fancy." She smiled and leaned in closer to him, "You know what you can get me? A horse,"

He smiled, "Alright. I should've known you would want a horse, silly girl. You can take the girl off the horse farm but you can't take the horse farm out of the girl." He tilted her chin up playfully with a flick of his finger.

# Chapter XXVIII

The red stallion bucked violently around the corral, half knocking the cowboy in charge of him down to the ground.

"I want that one." Violet said pointing to it.

Cyrus smiled. "Alright." he then shouted to the half-scared cowboy, "How much for the red stallion?"

"Thirty-five sir,"

Cyrus dug into his pants pocket to retrieve two bright and shining gold pieces, and gave them to the cowboy.

"Good luck riding him." The young cowboy said gravely as he picked up his hat and knocked the dust off of it.

Violet climbed the split-rail fence wearing her newly purchased riding skirt and landed in the corral. She walked up to the horse carefully. Its eyes and ears twitched as the stranger approached him. She gingerly, yet firmly placed a hand on its neck, and spoke some indistinguishable words in Cherokee and the horse seemed to relax for a moment. She grabbed onto its mane and slid onto the horse bareback. It bucked suddenly but she stayed on, throwing one arm up into the air for balance. It calmed after the first buck, and Violet whispered some more words in the horse's ear and its demeanor grew serene.

"This is a good horse." she said. She walked the horse out of the corral and turned to Cyrus. "Thank you. I have some business to take care of. I'll be back soon."

"What business could you have here in San Angelo?" Cyrus asked in disbelief.

"I need to talk to a friend of mine," she said, "I'll be back before supper."

"Alright," he agreed, but not happily to it. He had learned that once Violet made up her mind to do something it was nearly impossible to persuade her to do otherwise.

"I'll meet you at the hotel." she said as she kicked the horse into a gallop. The only thing on her mind right now was telling Billy about Edmund Forrester. The difficult thing would be to find him. He hadn't even told her where he might be staying, or where he was working. She would have to find out on her own.

She rode down Main Street and a poster in large marquee letters caught her eye. She dismounted so she could get a closer look. It was an announcement from the Federal Government claiming to give a $350 reward to any man who assisted the Ninth Cavalry in recovering the missing gold wages. Any men willing were to report to Fort Concho for duty.

This was a good place to start looking on her search. She knew that he was a duty bound individual, and had had personal experience with the stagecoach robbery. There wouldn't be a better man for the job. She knew that if she couldn't find him there to start looking around the stockyards and ranches for the cowboy. The red horse rode like lightning to Fort Concho.

It began to rain again. In the fort she could see several figures waiting outside of the adjutant's office, a small wooden building which operated as the headquarters. The first person she recognized was Jack from the stagecoach, his brown and red serape made him stand out in a crowd. She saw the familiar, rangy figure of Billy, standing in the rain with his old brown cowboy hat, rain falling off the brim like a waterfall. She rode up to the group with alarm and quickly dismounted. Jack recognized her with his knowing smile. Billy's eyes were large and bright with surprise.

"I need to talk to you, Billy." she spat out the words.

"Violet, what are you doing here?" his question was more from surprise rather than censure.

She pulled him to the side by his arm, and looked him in the eyes intently. "I have reason to believe that there is a gunman after you."

"What makes you think that?" he asked his eyes still wide-open still more surprised that she was there than he being a target for a gunman.

She lowered her voice to a whisper as not to alarm any of the other men and especially not the soldiers. "Because I read the letter that fell out of your saddlebag,"

"Why did you do that?" Billy asked.

Violet searched for some good reason, but couldn't find any explanation except for her natural curiosity.

"Never mind that—all I know is that Edmund Forrester is in town. I saw him on the street myself. Do you know that name?" She questioned, her panic-stricken eyes scanned his face.

"Sure do, most hated gunman west of the Mississippi." Billy said matter-of-factly.

After hearing this, tears began to well up in her eyes. She tried to hold them back. "Listen, you've got to be careful. I really think that the Smith's sent him after you, I just think…"

He stood there stoically until a smile of acceptance formed on his lips.

"I'll be alright. I'm riding with the Ninth Cavalry tomorrow, going to help them track down the stagecoach robbers. I don't think that even Mr. Forrester would try to lock horns with them." Billy put his hands on her soaking shoulders and lowered his voice, and focused deeply into her eyes. "I don't care about me, Violet. I don't want you to get hurt, if they see us together, he's liable to kill us both. I want you to stay away from here, away from me. Stay in town, and don't mention my name to anyone. Stay with Cyrus."

Those last three words hit her the hardest. Violet nodded, still trying to hold back the tears, but one managed to escape. She hoped that the pouring rain disguised it so that Billy would not see. There was no difference in expression in his placid face, he didn't seem to notice. He was so close to her at that moment. Her heart was beating fast in fear that this might be the last moment she would see him alive. His eyes were so clear. They both leaned closer to each other instinctively. Suddenly he pulled back, remembering her promise to another man. Billy would have to ride his own path. She couldn't be a part of it anymore.

"Alright," she spoke resignedly, "I best be going." She turned her head frantically and climbed back onto her horse. "I'll see you around, Billy." She managed to say hopefully in her faltering voice from atop her horse.

He simply nodded and tipped his hat to her slowly. The roar of thunder rolled across the dark prairie as she turned her horse toward San Angelo.

# Chapter XXIX

Violet rode back to the hotel, her new blouse and riding skirt were soaking wet and she was chilled to the bone. Her head was throbbing. She was haunted by the thought that Billy might die any day now. She knew that she couldn't stop Edmund Forrester, or the Smiths, herself. Even if she killed Forrester another gunman would be hired to take his place. She changed back into her green and white dress. She shivered as she sat on her bed and clutched the handle of her parasol.

She was supposed to meet Cyrus for supper. It was too early for that. She had to find something to do, something to distract her from this terrible news. She would try to find Cyrus and talk to him—that would make her feel better. Perhaps he would know of a way to stop Forrester.

How would she explain the situation to him? What was decorum worth now? She would just explain that Billy was a friend of hers who needed help. Maybe she was over-complicating things. Billy *would* be riding with the Ninth Cavalry for the next few days. Perhaps he would be safe like he had told her. Forrester wouldn't try anything in front of an entire regiment of soldiers. That gave her some comfort, but the threat lurked like a shadow in the back of her mind.

She knew the first place that Cyrus would be—the Lone Star saloon. She mustered some strength to her weary limbs and managed to walk down the hotel stairs and into the street to look for Cyrus.

She opened the canvas flap that served as a door to the musty smelling saloon. The warm glow of lamplight welcomed her in, and the smaller number of guests did not seem so scandalized at her appearance in the place. She ran the risk of becoming a fixture in this establishment. She didn't like the feeling of this saloon. Men at the bar sized her up. For the first time she noticed there were women working there. Many were dressed in immodestly garish outfits made of silk, and had hair accented with plumes of dyed ostrich and peacock feathers. She felt like a small wildflower among a garden of showy roses.

One particular woman with dark auburn hair glared at Violet with sharply slanted ice cold blue eyes, and looked her up and down. She wore a purple dress with a striped, tightly laced corset.

Violet found Cyrus alone with a bottle of whiskey. He was such a vivacious and social young man in Missouri, and wouldn't have been caught dead drinking alone, but that was the past.

He turned his head slowly when he heard the light click-clack of her heeled boots.

"Hello there," he said in a nonchalant way. He barely acknowledged her. Strangely, he did not pull out a chair for her like usual, but sat with his legs extended and boots crossed over one another. She sat down in the chair next to him stiffly. What was going on? Why was he drinking alone? This wasn't her Cyrus. She struggled to find something to say. She couldn't tell him about Billy, not when Cyrus was in this state.

"Are you alright?" she asked cautiously as she raised her eyebrows.

"I'm fine."

She could tell that he was lying. "What's wrong?" she asked, trying to be sympathetic.

"You don't understand the half of it, Violet."

"You can talk about it if you wish, you can tell me anything." she wanted him to explain why he was acting this way, but she was sincere with offering her listening ear to his troubles. She noticed the bottle of whiskey was already half-gone.

"You should never have come to Texas." he said, and took another swig from the bottle.

Her mouth hung open as she stared at him. This is not like anything she had expected him to say, "What are you talking about?" she said half in fear, "You have no idea of what I went through to get here!" she then said the rest in anger, incensed that he would say such a thing.

"You don't understand what I went through, Violet!"

Her heart was jerked back by this. Could it be the war he was speaking of? She turned her head away from him and was entirely frustrated at this point. He took another swig from the bottle and continued to speak, his speech only slightly slurred from the hard liquor. His stomach had grown hard from living out West. "I'm a liar Violet."

He was just rambling now, "What are you talking about, Cyrus? You're drunk. Maybe I should take you back to the hotel." she said, desperately trying to get out of this awful situation.

"Yes, I am drunk, but I need to tell you. I never had enough money for the ranch. Never. I shot Mr. Freeman because he wouldn't give me the money I needed, after all those days of sweat and blood on the trail. I thought I would finally have enough for the ranch that way. He shot me first. He died and I lived. I took the money he owed me from his wallet, I didn't steal an extra penny." His shaky glazed-over drunken eyes looked into hers. "All I wanted was to see you again, honey. I knew if I saw you before I died everything would be alright. But I lived. I never thought you would come, Violet. I never believed a word of it."

"What are you talking about? Are you saying that there was never a ranch, never even a possibility?"

He laughed wearily, and took another swig. "Yes my dear, that's exactly what I'm saying."

"You did lie to me." She half-whispered, and then she reached out and touched his arm. "But you told me you have money. You have the money now right? Things will work out..." she spoke the words but almost didn't believe them herself.

"No, I don't have it." he said, "But I'm sure I can win it back in a poker game tomorrow night."

"What do you mean win it back? Are you saying you lost the money you had before?"

Cyrus nodded sleepily and downed another shot of whiskey. He laughed again, it started as a chuckle but then escalated into something uproarious. "Yes, it's all gone!" he continued laughing until Violet had had enough of it and stamped out of the saloon.

She sat down wearily on the hotel bed. Seeing Cyrus that way disturbed her, she felt pity for him that he had sunk so low. Not only that, he had lied to her. The dream. The ranch. It was all a lie.

But maybe he was right, maybe he could win it back in the poker game. Cyrus had always been an excellent poker player, beating out the toughest competition in Missouri. Why was he doing this now? Why had he toyed with the very thing he had promised her? Perhaps he just wasn't in his right mind and felt overconfident when he bet the money for the ranch. After his accident things were probably very painful for him, maybe that's why he lost in the poker game, he was weak.

Violet didn't know anything anymore. One of the reasons for her coming to Texas was gone, all fake. That hopeful promise written in the letter, of a home that both of them could share, it was all a lie.

That entire day had been a blur, not only the shocking revelations from Cyrus, but the fact that Billy's life was in danger. There was nothing she could do about either. For once in her life she felt entirely helpless to amend the situations she was faced with. She crashed on her bed with a pounding headache that would seem to split her skull in two as hot tears rolled down her face.

# Chapter XXX

Billy stepped out into the early morning sunlight, from his canvas tent just outside the grounds of Fort Concho. Some of the itinerant volunteers had been granted tent lodging while they helped the soldiers recover the missing wages. A pleasant pocket of chilled air greeted his face. It was morning on the Texas prairie. He missed his home nestled in the Hill Country, though he didn't thoroughly admit it. He missed the sprawling oak trees and rolling hills. He would stay here long enough to earn enough money to make the journey back. He would leave the fort, San Angelo, and Violet behind. He tried not to think about her. As long as she was engaged to Cyrus she was unattainable. It wasn't right to take another man's woman in his book, although he still loved her.

On the horizon he saw a single rider on a white steed. Billy grabbed his gun belt from atop his cot, and slung it around his hips. It couldn't hurt to be cautious. His tent-mate, Jack, was still snoring loudly. He kicked his cot to get his companion to wake, but it was ineffective. Billy stepped out of the tent, his hand hovering readily over the butt of his pistol. The rider approached steadily. As he came closer Billy could discern that he was not riding a horse after all, but a white mule.

He knew of only one person that rode a snow-white mule, and that was Fortunato. His normally roguish black and gold sombrero was tattered and torn, and his general appearance was of a man defeated and exhausted.

Why was he here? He couldn't possibly know that Billy would be at the fort. Billy wondered if he would try something else like he had done at Puerta de Chana. He wouldn't let him get away with his gun or his horse again.

"Buenos Dias," Fortunato said grimly, not expecting to see Billy again.

"What are you doing here?" Billy asked gravely.

Fortunato reached up and slowly took off his sombrero, as not to alarm Billy. "I know you don't want to trust me, señor…"

"Just say it,"

"I did not know you would be here. I come to speak to the cavalry."

"Are ya fixin' on turning yourself in?"

"No señor. It is not about that. I am no longer one of them."

Billy was confused, what was Fortunato saying? He was no longer a bandido? He just couldn't believe it.

"What do you mean you ain't a bandido no more?"

"Señor, es no importante. My sister Lupe was taken from mi casa. I think she was sold to the Comanche, by that bastard who I used to call my friend—Armando."

Billy stared at him wide-eyed and confused. Armando was a Comanchero? It now made a lot of sense, why he had stolen their horses why he was looking over Violet like a trinket to be bought and sold. Why else would Fortunato travel all the way to Fort Concho if his sister had not been kidnapped? He had even put himself in danger if the Buffalo Soldiers discovered he had been a bandido and worked with the Comancheros. Although, since he had worked with a now known Comanchero he would make a good scout.

"Why did he take her?" Billy said.

"He was angry señor. He wanted my sister to marry him, but she refused. He is evil, señor. He has un corazon del diablo! He does not love her, and since she does not love him he sold her. I must find my sister, señor, before she is lost forever."

Billy actually felt pity for the wandering Fortunato. He thought about how horrible it would be if his own sister, Junie, had been kidnapped and sold to the Comanche. If the

Comanche and the Bandidos were cooperating with each other, it was his duty to inform the Ninth Cavalry.

"Alright, I am sorry about what happened to your sister, Lupe. I'll tell the sergeant your story."

A smile lit up Fortunato's weary face, "Gracias, señor."

Billy marched up to the fort. Fortunato began to follow him, but he put up a hand to stop him.

"I'll tell them myself." He knew that the soldiers would trust him over a former bandido.

As Billy was about ready to knock on Sergeant Hopkins's office door a young soldier, a scout, came barreling in on horseback from the southwest. He and his horse were breathing heavily, and from his sweating and furrowed brow Billy could tell there was something wrong. Sergeant Hopkins came out of his office as the young soldier dismounted. The scout saluted hastily. "Sir, there are reports out near Tankersley of Comanche kidnappings and attacks on homesteaders. At least one home burned, sir."

The sergeant looked down thoughtfully for a moment, this would be just another problem to worry about, but it was his duty to protect the local settlers. He looked up quickly with bright eyes.

"Thank you private. Take care of your horse. We will be heading out as soon as possible."

"Yes, sir." the private responded, out of breath.

Billy spoke up as the sergeant almost passed his shoulder, "Sir, I know I volunteered to help find the missing wages, but I would like to ride out. I have some information that you might find useful."

"Go on," The sergeant looked interested.

"I think the bandidos are working with the Comanche. A young woman from Puerta de Chana was kidnapped and sold to them. Do you think there might be some connection?"

"Hmm, quite possibly; the Comanche have been buying and selling souls for years, sometimes from other tribes. Who told you about this young woman?" His dark eyes searched Billy's face.

"Just someone I know, sir. He's right outside the fort. It was his sister."

He waved Billy off with his hand, "Alright, tell him to come along too. We'll need all the help we can get.

"Yes sir." Billy couldn't help but smile, he was going to help someone. He ran back to the tent to inform Fortunato.

Fortunato stood next the tent, his head hung low as he clutched his sombrero to his chest.

"Hola, señor. What news?"

"They'll let you come. The soldiers will be riding out any minute now." Billy barged into the tent. Jack was now sitting on his cot, smoking a cigar.

"What's that feller doing out there, friend of yours?"

"The soldiers are riding out. We're going after the Comanche."

"Now why the hell are we doing that for?" he said as he dropped his smoking cigar in his lap, and his hands scrambled to pick it up.

"Comanche have been attacking the homesteaders." Billy said as he picked up his saddlebags and reloaded his gun.

"Alright," Jack said reluctantly, cigar now in hand as he shook his head, "I should've been in Santa Fe by now..." he mumbled as he put on his wide-brimmed hat. Jack walked out of the tent and readied his cast-off horse from the Fort.

"Hope this thing doesn't die before we get to wherever we're going. For heaven sakes! Poor thing is malnourished and bowlegged. You can tell the rest of the army don't give a shit about the Buffalo Soldiers..." Jack mumbled from his cigar-laden mouth.

"Well, whatever happens I ain't giving you my Apache horse. It's done right good so far."

"Hmm," Jack grunted as he tightened up the cinch on the saddle.

All three men rode up to the Fort to meet with the soon-to-depart troop. Fortunato's eyes darted about nervously as the sergeant approached them.

"Hello. Are you the man whose sister was captured and sold to the Comanche?"

"Sí, señor."

"We'll need your help in tracking the Comanche down. Did you ever have ties with the Comancheros?" Fortunato looked down at the ground, reluctant to speak. "Speak up young man!" The sergeant said, "We haven't got all day."

"Sí, señor. It is true. I used to work for their leader, but did not know he sold to the Comanche. I was just a simple thief—I did not want to hurt anyone."

"Fine. I can tell that you need our help or you wouldn't have come this far to get it. As long as you help with the scouting and fighting you are on good terms with US government."

With the sound of, "Move out!" the entire troop of the well-polished, put-together Ninth Cavalry and the three extra ragged volunteers all rode out to the southwest to investigate the attacks on the settlers.

# Chapter XXXI

That last night Violet had fallen asleep without eating supper with Cyrus. Her stomach growled with a vengeance. Her head pounded, and seemed to punish her for crying the night before. As she woke up the first thoughts in her head were, *tonight's the night that Cyrus wins back the money in the poker game.* She didn't want to think about it at all, but she couldn't help it.

The blue sky greeted her from outside her hotel window. She wondered where Billy might be, and if he was safe. So far she had not seen him since she warned him about Edmund Forrester. That was a terrible night. Things were not turning out the way she had planned them. Cyrus should never have lost the money for the ranch, and they should've already been married. Her life was moving slowly, more slowly than she would have liked.

She didn't even know her fiancé anymore, with the drinking and incessant gambling, he was a changed man. But perhaps if he won the money on this one last poker game she could get him to quit for good, to settle down and earn an honest living. Violet did not wholly object to gambling, but she only approved of it as recreation to be enjoyed only occasionally, and definitely didn't think it should be pursued as a career.

She spent the morning alone, in a restaurant, over a plate of hoecakes. Part of her wished she was back home in Missouri, and that she had never made the journey to Texas—although she knew that was a lie.

\* \* \*

It was a good fifteen miles to Tankersley, and Billy wondered what they might find there. Ever since he was a child he had heard the stories of the children taken from their homes, their fathers scalped and their mothers raped. He knew that the Comanche were the fiercest Indians on the plains, making war with anyone and everyone. To make it worse they were the fastest and most skilled horsemen, even rivaling the Lipan Apache. They had become one of the first tribes to adopt the use of the rifle, and even though they had them, they didn't need them. They could fire twenty arrows while a white man could make off one shot. It had gotten worse since the US government was trying to round them up, and put them on reservations. Since then, the total rage of the Comanche was unleashed and homesteaders lived in constant fear of violent raids.

Billy hoped that there would be some settlers still alive, who had managed to hide in their cellars or under their beds. It was almost better to be killed than to be captured by the Comanche. They enslaved their prisoners and forced them to do hard labor while they were torturously lashed and beaten. He wondered if Lupe had already met that fate.

The company of Buffalo soldiers and the three volunteers rode over the vast and lonely prairie until they could see the billowing, death grey cloud of smoke over the small settlement of Tankersley. The entire troop rode faster to reach the victims—if there were any victims left to save. The large cabin was half burnt and left with a gaping, cavernous hole. Dark smoke was still rising from the embers of what used to be walls. Bits of torn calico, pots and pans, and bags of cornmeal were strewn over the blackened prairie grass. The sergeant dismounted to investigate.

"Look for survivors!" he ordered. Billy and Jack went inside the charred mass that used to be a house to investigate. There was no sign of anyone. Billy found a family Bible still resting on the shelf with only the binding and cover slightly burnt. He carefully opened it up, the name Tankersley was written on the title page.

"Sir?" he showed the open Bible to the sergeant.

The sergeant's eyes grew wide with concern. "They attacked the first settlers in this area. The Tankersley's had been on good terms with the Indians for years…"

The Comanche were becoming even more indiscriminate with their attacks. As Billy was about ready to get back into his Apache saddle, his ears perked up. He heard a very faint sound, almost like a cat mewing. Out of the corner of his eye he noticed the blackened cellar door for the first time. He opened the hatches and ran down the stairs. The sound grew louder and he could tell it was a child crying and sniffling. Between the jams and potatoes he saw a small boy of about four or five years old with blond hair, sitting in the dirt. He sniffed, "I want my mommy."

Billy picked him up and put him on his shoulder, the little boy wailed and hit at him frantically. Billy walked back up the stairway, and from the open cellar door he could see the silhouette of the sergeant waiting.

"What did you find?"

"A little boy," Billy quickly handed the squirming child having a tantrum to the sergeant. Once the boy was safe within the soldier's strong arms he began to calm down and his cries turned to stifled sucked-in air and sniffles. The sergeant looked uncomfortable with the boy soaking his tears into his blue coat, but when he tried to tug him away he cried even more. The little boy stuck to him like a barnacle on the hull of a great ship.

Fortunato was off his mule and tracing the ground for clues to where the Comanche might have been last.

"Señor," he called to the sergeant, "I believe that the Comanche have gone to the east." He pointed to a patch of grass that had been trampled by horses, also there was a bonnet lying on the ground, perhaps belonging to the stranded boy's mother.

"We head east. Move out!" The sergeant ordered.

The sun was sinking lower in the sky. Billy hoped that they would reach the Comanche and the captives by sunset. The Comanche were masters of stealth warfare and knew the land. Even the Ninth Cavalry would be no match to the Indians come nightfall.

* * *

A nervous pit grew in Violet's stomach as the hour of Cyrus's poker game approached. It would be held at 6 o'clock at one of the more respectable establishments, a combination restaurant, saloon and gambling house, called the Painted Parrot. She had hardly seen or spoken to Cyrus that day, only to ask when and where the game was to take place. The ticking clock on the wall of the hotel lobby seemed to heighten her anxiety. It was five minutes till the game. The fate of her dream rested in the dirty hands of gamblers nestled among brightly colored chips.

She decided that she would watch it. She knew the rules of poker after observing her father and his friends play many times at their house. Perhaps if she was there Cyrus would take the odds more seriously.

She splashed some cold water on her face to calm herself before she went to the lobby of the Painted Parrot. It was a large, sprawling building. Men crowded around the spinning white, black and red colors of roulette wheels. Dealers presided over Faro and three card Monte, while the gamblers slouched anxiously over their cards. The bouncing roulette balls, the clinking of glasses, and shuffling cards and fiddle was the music of the hall. There was a thin stairway that led up to the second floor of the establishment, which was partitioned by a blue velvet curtain fringed with gold.

The bright green felt poker tables that dotted the large room stood in sharp contrast with the red and black ornate floral patterned carpet. Cyrus was already there and greeted her with his disarming smile.

"Come, my dear. Sit by me." He pulled out a chair for her this time and swept his panama hat down gracefully. He was dressed differently now. He wore a black suit with a white silk vest and black string tie. He had shaved, the stubble was gone and his overgrown mustache was neatly trimmed back to its original form. He reminded her of how he looked back home in Missouri. He once again carried the charm of a true southern gentleman.

"The other players, or perhaps one might say, my opponents, are about to arrive." He paused for a moment. "I'm sorry about last night my dear. I wasn't in my right mind. Do forgive me."

He was acting completely different from the night before. His ranting and his crudeness were gone. All of his politeness and suavity were back. Violet wasn't sure if she should forgive him, he said some awful things to her that night—things that might not be easily forgiven. Perhaps he was just drunk and talking nonsense. Without realizing what she was saying, she spoke, "Alright, I do forgive you."

Cyrus smiled, broad and beaming.

A plump middle-aged man sat down at the table. He wore a white hat with an elaborate band, and a cream colored suit with a purple satin vest.

"Good evening Mr. Weatherby." Cyrus said.

"Howdy. Is she playing?" Mr. Weatherby asked as he pointed toward Violet.

"No sir, she's just going to be my good luck charm."

"Well, that's an unfair advantage!" he said, and laughed heartily, revealing several missing teeth.

From the din in the hall she managed to pick out the sound of the doors creaking open, and Violet turned her head to see in horror a person she recognized. He wore the same wide brimmed black felt hat and two pistols that sat cross-draw on his hips. To add to his already large intimidating figure was his white fur-coat.

"How do you do gentlemen?" Edmund Forrester said, "I'm here for a game of poker, I trust you are all here for the same reason?" he spoke with the smoothness of the British aristocracy.

"Yes, sir." Mr. Weatherby said without hesitation.

"Indeed." Cyrus said.

"Excellent. Where are the other players?" He placed his jacket on the back of his chair and sat down in a fluid motion. Once he sat down Violet noticed a familiar revolver with the mark CSA in one of the holsters. That was Billy's gun, the one Jasper had taken from him outside of Deer Creek. That's when she knew for certain Edmund Forrester was the man who was sent to kill Colton. Unfortunately she had left her gun in her room. It was a decision she regretted. If she had it, she might not have hesitated to kill him. Still, if she killed him sitting at the poker table it would've been murder. There was nothing she could do. Her hands were tied. She tried to shake off the shocked look of hatred off her face with a forced smile.

"May I be introduced to the lovely lady? Will she be participating in the game?"

Cyrus cleared his throat, "This is Miss Violet Corntassel, soon to be my wife. She won't be playing this evening."

"How do you do Miss Violet?" he said with the oiliness of a snake.

"Fine, thank you." Violet said. She had to force out those words, she couldn't stand being in his presence, let alone tolerate his smarmy compliments, and the way he looked at her.

A dusty cowpoke sashayed down the skinny stairway with a giggling saloon girl trailing behind. He took a seat between Mr. Weatherby and Violet. Violet looked up and she saw another unexpected arrival, it was the woman she had seen the other day at the Lone Star saloon. Her dark auburn hair was tied up in a bun and she wore a longer, more respectable version of the dress Violet had seen her in before. The woman's cold blue eyes looked at her squint-eyed. Violet hadn't even met this woman, why was she already treating her with disdain and hatred?

"May I join you gentlemen?" she said every word with a phony sense of propriety.

"Please, Miss Jeannine," said Mr. Weatherby. She situated herself between Mr. Weatherby and the cowpoke.

Jeannine leaned across the table, "Cyrus. How are you?"

She knew Cyrus? Violet looked over at him, shocked. Cyrus's jaw tightened and he said nothing.

"Let's get going! I haven't got all night." Mr. Weatherby said.

Violet started to wonder about this woman she had seen in the bar and that happened to appear at the poker game. Who was Jeannine? How did she know Cyrus? It was all a very curious matter. Surely she could not know him well.

Edmund Forrester shuffled the cards with a quick hand and dealt five cards to each player. "Five card draw gentlemen," he said then glanced at Jeannine, "and lady."

Violet could tell that Cyrus's cards were not the best, but he had a poker face that others would kill for. He only had a pair of twos, a queen, a four and a seven. It all depended on the draw round. Violet looked at each of the players faces trying to detect tells. The cowpoke scratched his head as he looked at his cards. Jeannine just glared back at her when she glanced her way, so Violet went onto the next player. Mr. Weatherby's face grew red as he held his breath in. Edmund Forrester coolly leaned back in his chair, with excessive nonchalance. He leaned forward again and tapped the green-felted table twice with his brown eyes peeping from his smug, square face. He must have a good hand.

Cyrus bet two dollars to get the ball rolling, and play continued. The cowpoke pushed his chips closer to the center of the table to see the bet. Jeannine, without glancing at her cards, saw and raised the bet to five dollars. Mr. Weatherby hesitantly saw the five dollars. Forrester called the bet.

The draw phase began and the dealership passed to Cyrus. He discarded two of his cards, the four and the seven. It was a risky move to hold onto the twos. The top card was burned and he took two more off the deck. It was a lucky draw, a queen and a two. Full house. Sweat grew on the cowpoke's forehead "I'll take one card."

Jeannine didn't draw any new cards. Mr. Weatherby drew three new cards.

"I bet twenty." Cyrus said.

The cowpoke reluctantly called.

"I see the bet and raise it by forty." Jeannine said. There was a gasp from around the table. She cast a glare toward Cyrus and Violet. If Violet didn't know any better Jeannine was jealous. Maybe she was just a strange woman.

"Sorry folks," Mr. Weatherby said, "too rich for my blood. These cards can't take it. I got to fold."

Forrester raised the bet even further to eighty dollars. Cyrus saw the bet and raised it by twenty.

"Are you sure that isn't too high for you sir?" Forrester goaded Cyrus.

"You don't know me yet, Mr. Forrester."

Though she disdained Forrester's comment, the stakes were even higher now, and Violet worried that Cyrus's cards weren't good enough.

It was time for the showdown. The cowpoke was the first to show his cards, a pair of aces and a queen kicker. Jeannine then splayed out her cards on the table. To everyone's surprise she only had a pair of threes with a high card ace. Why had she bet so much with cards that didn't even stand a chance? Forrester showed his cards, with a satisfied grin—a pair of jacks and a pair of tens. Then Cyrus showed his hand: full house with three twos and queens.

"I do say sir that I am surprised. I thought you were bluffing to impress the ladies."

A half-smile formed on Cyrus's face. "Mr. Forrester, chock it up to gut instinct, or luck if you'd rather."

Cyrus raked in the chips, all of the nearly three-hundred dollars' worth.

Violet could see that Forrester was getting irritated. His square jaw tightened and he distanced himself from the table a bit, by resting his arm on his cane. What if Cyrus really angered him and he would try something?

Violet leaned into Cyrus's ear, "Perhaps you should quit the game…"

"No darling," he said in her ear, and then addressed the whole table, "One more round gentlemen?" Jeannine sneered at this comment— he had intentionally left her out.

"I have to go." Jeannine said as she picked her blue shawl up from the back of the chair, Mr. Weatherby began to protest. "It was nice playing with you all." Those ice blue eyes shot a furious glance at Cyrus and then to Violet before she dashed to the gambling house doors.

Violet knew something was wrong—something in her gut told her. Why had this woman been so cold and hateful to her, to someone she didn't even know? She was going to find out.

"Excuse me, I'm going to get some fresh air." She made her way to the exit and stood outside on the boardwalk. Though she had half-expected it, she was surprised and maybe little startled when she saw the tall, intimidating figure of Jeannine standing in the shadows. How was she going to confront her? She knew what she thought—she didn't know how to say it.

"I couldn't help but notice…" Violet began.

"That I don't like you?"

Violet turned to face her directly, "Well, I wasn't going to say—"

"Oh, I saw those little wheels turning in that head of yours. I was sizing you up. I wanted to know what kind of woman you were."

"But you don't even know who I am."

"Of course I do." her words spilled out like venomous honey, "The first time I met Cyrus all he ever talked about was you."

A black needle pierced Violet's heart. She mustered all the strength she had left in her voice. "So you do know Cyrus."

Jeannine laughed light-heartedly, which annoyed Violet. "Oh you don't know the half of it honey. Cyrus is mine. He might have loved you so very long ago, but he's mine now. Truly, I'm the only one who can understand what he went through. While you were making you're little journey down here to Texas I was here for him. After a while he stopped talking about you, you see."

All the rage and anger Violet had ever felt burned inside of her ten-fold, and her fingers curled up into her palm. She drew her entire shoulder back and landed a punch solidly on her perfectly straight, lily-white nose. She heard the crunch of bone. Jeannine's boot heels clicked as she staggered back. She held her blue shawl up to her nose, streaming blood.

"You crazy bitch..." Jeannine choked out.

"If you ever tell me filthy lies like that again I'll kill you." Violet's dark eye's glinted and fear finally entered Jeannine's impenetrable ice blue eyes. Violet stomped back inside the saloon fighting back tears as she went. Surely, this Jeannine, whoever she was, was a liar. Violet took a seat solidly next to Cyrus.

"Feeling better?" Cyrus said pleasantly as he looked up from his poker hand fanned in front of him.

"Yes, thank you." she said.

# Chapter XXXII

The sun had already begun to set; light pink and orange rays cast long shadows on the prairie grass. Billy's heart beat faster as worry loomed large that they might not make it to the Comanche camp by sundown. The horses were exhausted from the long ride. Billy hadn't seen Jack for a while. He turned his head around to see that Jack was lagging far behind, and trying his best to keep the poor pony he was riding moving.

Sergeant Hopkins raised his hand in an order to stop. A scout came speedily from up ahead to meet the rest of the troop.

"Sir," the scout said, "I believe the Comanche camp is less than a quarter mile up the trail."

"You believe, or do you know, corporal?" the sergeant responded.

"I know sir. Barely escaped them,"

Sergeant Hopkins's eyes grew worried, "Did they see you?"

"No sir." the corporal said with self-assurance.

The command was given and the soldiers and the volunteers continued onward toward the Comanche camp.

Billy could see the tipis over the horizon, smoke still burned from a fire. Several horses were tied to stakes outside, and many more hundreds were grazing on the outskirts of the village. Many of those horses dispersed as Comanche warriors took hold of the saddles and prepared for the attack. Startled warriors dropped what they were doing and grabbed their feathered shields, raised their war-lances, and armed their bows. Instead of waiting for the cavalry to reach their village the twenty or so Braves rode full-onward at a gallop. Horses weaved around the Buffalo Soldiers. The whizzing of arrows and the irregular pattern of gunfire followed. The corporal fell back onto his horse as an arrow pierced his shoulder.

A warrior rode hanging from the side of his saddle, firing arrows at the cavalry as he went. The sergeant fired one shot with his pistol, killing the pinto which subsequently fell on top of the brave, crushing him to death. At the sight and sound of one of their own being killed the Comanche ceased firing and pulled back to the village. They knew that their numbers were few, and would rather live to fight another day. It was their way of surrender, they just didn't use a white flag. The sergeant led the rest of the soldiers into the camp, and dismounted.

"Check the camp for captives, I want everyone recovered!"

The three volunteers dismounted their horses near one of the tipis. Billy felt incredibly uncomfortable with the Comanche warriors so close, he felt that an arrow would be sticking out of his back at any moment so he kept his finger near the trigger. A single shot rang out behind the tipi, barely missing Fortunato's ear. Fortunato turned around discovering that Armando and other Comancheros were cowering behind the tipi next to a large pile of rifles they had pilfered, and moments before had sold to the Comanche.

Armando spat at Fortunato and cursed him in Spanish as the Buffalo Soldiers swarmed the outlaws, and carried him away.

"You traitor—you will die for what you have done to me!"

Fortunato coolly replied, "You are the traitor, señor. You will rot in hell for what you did to my sister."

Jack and Billy flung the buffalo skin door to the tipi open. About ten captives, all women and children huddled together inside. One girl with dark eyes looked up at her rescuers. The back of her dress had been ripped open, and her back was scabbed and bloody from lashings. She smiled a weak smile and crossed herself. It was Lupe. Jack rushed inside to help her because she was too weak to stand.

"Hola señorita, he venido a ayudarte." He placed her like a sack of flour over his shoulder and put her gently on his horse. Billy ushered the others out, many were wounded. Several were malnourished and looked as though they had been with the Comanche for quite some time. The sergeant rushed over to help the other captives out. He reached his hand into the darkness. One woman with frazzled yellow hair and a smudged face looked up. Billy recognized her as Maybelle, the woman from the stagecoach. Her hand drew back, but then realizing the predicament she was in she took the sergeant's hand. As she walked into the sunlight she could see her son clinging to Sergeant Hopkins's shoulder. Just a few days ago she might have yelled and screamed and protested that a black man, let alone a soldier of the Union was holding her son. That didn't matter anymore. She looked up to the sergeant and her round eyes began to well with tears.

"God Bless you sir." Maybelle said, "You found my little boy—I thought he was lost forever. I can't thank you enough."

The sergeant handed the calm boy down to his mother, and she wept into his straw colored hair.

"Have all the captives been recovered?" The sergeant demanded, turning around to second in command.

"Yes sir." he replied.

"Bind the prisoners. Put the wounded on horseback. Gather up those rifles."

Armando and two other Comancheros gave their captors difficulty. They were tied together and forced to walk behind the rear horse. Lupe smiled from atop Jack's horse in satisfaction that Armando and the other Comancheros would finally see justice. Fortunato took off his hat and walked up to his sister—his head hung low. He was not sure what to say; he was certain that she would forever be ashamed of him. He looked to the ground in humility with puppy-like eyes.

He began to speak in Spanish, "I am sorry sister. I failed you, I did not know that he would try to do such a thing. I should never have let him in my house."

Lupe sat stoically for a moment looking off into the distance, and then turned to see her brother.

"It is alright, my brother." she said, "All is well now. The saints teach us to forgive. So I forgive you."

Fortunato nodded and slowly backed away to get on his own horse.

The corporal who had been shot earlier had already removed the arrow from his shoulder himself. As Billy had his foot in the stirrup, about ready to mount the black and white Apache pony he could see from the corner of his eye a familiar brown quarter horse, standing right next to a yellow appaloosa. His saddle and tack were still there, safe and sound.

"Sir," Billy called to the sergeant, "This is my horse."

"What evidence do you have to support your claim?" he inquired.

Billy examined the back haunch for the family brand, CR. It was there. "This is my brand."

"Alright, you may retake it." He then spoke an order to the troop, "Round up any stolen horses. They are now the property of the US government."

The soldiers rounded up approximately two-hundred horses from the Comanche camp. Billy wondered if it was the right thing to do. Sure, the Comancheros had been stealing and selling horses to the Comanche for years, but maybe some of them had legitimately belonged to the Indians, taken out of the wild plains and tamed. It didn't matter now, the order had been given and carried out. Besides, the Ninth Cavalry needed those horses as badly as anyone.

* * *

The night ended with Cyrus splitting the final pot of one-hundred and fifty dollars with Forrester. Thankfully, Cyrus did not win the whole pot which left Forrester's pride undamaged, and more importantly, Cyrus's life was still intact. There was no sign of Jeannine, much to Violet's relief. She never wanted to see that woman again.

As Violet and Cyrus were walking back to the hotel he jingled his newfound fortune in his deep pockets.

"You know Violet," he said with a smile, "I told you that I would make it all better with the poker game. You just had to have a little faith in me." He put his arm around her shoulder.

She stopped in her tracks. "What? Do you mean to tell me that you have enough money for the ranch?"

Cyrus smiled broadly as he turned to face her. "That's exactly what I mean dearest."

Violet stepped back a foot. "Wait, how could you have enough money for five-hundred acres just from your winnings tonight? Why, you only have about three-seventy…"

"I am more prepared than that my dear. Do you think that I could have wasted all my money?

I am more shrewd a gambler than that, honey."
He chuckled to himself.

A glimmer of hope kindled in Violet's heart and traveled up to shine from her face. The dream was still alive. It also meant that what Cyrus had said before behind the whiskey bottle were alcohol induced lies. She smiled and wrapped her arms around him.

"Now that you have the money," she said as she stepped back, "will you promise me to quit gambling?"

Cyrus's face grew dark. "Of course, yes my dear."

He kissed her goodnight on the cheek before they both retired to their separate rooms.

Violet extinguished the lamp and before she closed her eyes she thought about Jeannine, and the awful things she had heard from her that night. A dark thought crept into her heart—could there be any truth in them? Surely, this was a woman with a shady reputation and not to be trusted. Perhaps she was jealous of her and Cyrus. No one could ever know her motives. Violet satisfied herself with that answer for the moment and fell in a deep, restful sleep.

* * *

Billy and Jack were given the assignment to drive the horses back to Fort Concho. They had the most experience cowboying, so they were natural choices. Billy hadn't been on a drive in what seemed like ages so he jumped at the chance. He had loaned his Apache pony out to Jack whose previously borrowed horse was now ridden by Lupe. They stayed back behind the troop of Buffalo Soldiers

Billy was glad to have his familiar mare back. She was sturdy and he was used to riding her. She remembered him when he had retaken her from the Comanche. She was no worse for the wear and seemed well-fed, but was in need of a good brushing. He hoped to borrow the stables at the fort.

Lupe, though torn and tattered from her time in captivity assisted them with the driving of the nearly two-hundred wild horses. They could hear her yell in Spanish as she rounded up a stray colt. Billy noticed Jack watching her.

"Quite a girl, huh?" Billy said.

"Yep…" Jack responded still looking at her riding in the moonlight. "She's a survivor. Ain't met no stronger woman. Prays like a saint too—never lets go of those rosary beads."

"You talked to her?" Billy said.

"Yeah, good thing my Spanish is up to par. Nearly talked my ear off." He paused as if he was thinking. "She told me she's tired of living with her brother in Puerta de Chana. I don't blame her, considering what's happened to her." He took a deep breath, "I'm thinking about taking her with me to Santa Fe, if she's up to it."

Billy feigned surprise. "Have you asked her yet?"

"Nope. Was planning on doing so when got to town but…"

"But what?"

"Well, I never saw myself as the marrying kind, to settle down and have a family and such… I think she may have changed my mind." Jack chomped on a new cigar, "You got a girl, pard?"

"Not yet." Billy shook his head with a smirk.

"What about that one half-breed that had accompanied you on the stagecoach? I figured she had taken a shine to you."

"You figured wrong, pard. Turns out she came all this way to meet her fiancé in San Angelo. I don't even cross her mind."

Jack nodded in mock agreement, "That tweren't what I saw. You think you got her pegged, but you ain't."

Jack shot off in the direction of Lupe to help her round up a stray. She had the situation under control, but Billy assumed that Jack used it as a technique to be nearer to her.

The moon hung high and the stars began to appear in the wide, purple, prairie sky. Billy wondered where Violet was right now, probably asleep, he reckoned. Maybe she was dreaming. He thought about what Jack had said. He was wrong about one thing, Billy couldn't quite grasp a firm understanding of Violet's mind, so mysterious and guarded as it was. Besides, even if there were any truth to Jack's suspicions, Violet could never turn her back on Cyrus. Not now, now that she had come so far.

He thought about some of the other girls back home. There was Bonnie Sue who had taken a shine to him; sixteen, blonde curls and a head as empty as a bucket in a dry well during a drought in the middle of summer. Nobody was like Violet, nobody. She was smart and had instincts about things. Most of the other girls he met never could've done what she did. Cross the country all the way from Missouri to Texas, alone. Cyrus was a lucky man, he thought. He believed that Cyrus didn't deserve her. No one he knew deserved her.

# Chapter XXXIII

Upon waking, Violet dressed herself in her new riding outfit and pulled on her old boots. She knocked on Cyrus's door to see if he was in, but no one answered. The light of dawn still hadn't crept over the horizon and she wondered where he could so early in the morning. She went downstairs and gobbled up her breakfast of hoecakes, bacon, and coffee.

She had been looking forward to a visit to the stable where her new horse was residing. It had been a day since she rode the red stallion, and she wanted to make sure that the fiery red steed remembered its new owner. Besides, she wouldn't mind a ride outside of town on the plains, and the horse would sure appreciate the exercise. Before she reached the stable she stopped in Veck's general store for some horse goodies. She couldn't decide if the horse would prefer apples, carrots or oats so she bought one bag of each. With goods in hand she made her way down to the stable.

As she was about to go inside she heard two men talking in hushed voices. She looked through the slats of the wooden door and couldn't make out their faces, but it looked as though they were having some sort of disagreement.

"...you told me you would, Snake Eyes."

Violet held back a gasp, one of the men in the argument was the leader in the stagecoach robbery.

"I'm sorry Roger, I can't. I'll have the money for you in a few weeks after this next job." Snake Eyes replied.

"You better make good on your promise, or else…"

"Or else what?"

"I'm tired of waiting around. You know what else." Roger said and then walked out the side door of the stable. Violet rushed over to the opposite side of the stable as not to be discovered by Snake Eyes—he might recognize her. The front doors creaked open. A man with a lanky build and dark hair stepped out of the stable. He was wearing a nice suit and put on his panama hat to shield his eyes from the sun. A small twig cracked under her heel as she leaned back. He turned his head, alarmed by the noise.

It was Cyrus.

His green eyes shrewdly investigated the scene, but he could not see her from that angle. He walked on down the street and back to the hotel. Violet was breathing heavily. How could Cyrus be Snake Eyes? It could not be true. Could there have been more than two men in the stable? Only two had walked out. She ventured a peek inside. It was empty and still except for the baying of horses.

She knew that Cyrus might check her hotel room to visit her. Panicked, she realized that he couldn't know she had visited the stable. Where could she go? Frantically she ran behind the livery building. She realized she still had the bags of oats, apples and carrots. That would certainly give her away. She hid them beneath a shrub near the corral and hurriedly walked past several buildings until she dumped out on the end of Main Street. She was next to the combination clothing and jewelry store, so she slipped inside. She tried to make it look like she was casually shopping. Behind a tree of bonnets she tried to catch her breath. She grabbed ahold of the one closest to her, and began a mock inspection. This one was quite ugly. It was made of yellow-green taffeta with a smattering of silk flowers, which if real, would've looked wilted and dead.

The small brass bell above the shop door tinkled. She turned her head to see who it was.

It was him, Cyrus. She quickly put the bonnet on her head to cover face which was growing pale.

"Well hello," she said nonchalantly as she glanced at herself in the small mirror.

"Hello there. You weren't at the hotel so I was wondering where you might be so early..." he said.

"Oh, just doing a little shopping. What do you think?"

"I think its hideous darling. What have you done with your senses?" He teased and took the bonnet off her head and placed it back on the rack.

Her heart raced in fear that he might discover where she had been. "Well," she said, "It isn't proper for a lady to go out without a bonnet."

"Since when did you ever care about that?" A wolf-like grin formed on his lips.

"Who says I don't now?"

His eyes traveled up and down her figure. "Yes, you in your riding skirt and boots..."

Violet flushed in worry that she had been discovered. "I was getting tired of wearing those hoop skirts, you know I'm more comfortable like this anyway." She hoped that that answer would do.

"Yes," he said with a smile, "That's why I love you."

Violet forced out a smile. At least she had been able to fool him into thinking she really had been out shopping.

"Come meet me at the Cantina down the street, I believe it's called Rosita's." She nodded, she had no other choice. "Until later dear." he said, and kissed her on the cheek. As he left she picked up another bonnet to perpetuate the charade.

What would Cyrus do if he discovered that she knew the truth about him, his alias, the fact that he was a robber and an outlaw?

She hated herself for not recognizing Snake Eyes as Cyrus in the first place. But how could she have known? She hadn't seen Cyrus in more than five years. The mind alters our memories of faces. Besides, they did all have bandannas over their faces to disguise themselves. What clue did she have except for those green eyes? There were plenty of men with green eyes, she reasoned.

The fact was she knew now. Had he seen her so many days ago outside of San Angelo? He might suspect that she knows. She couldn't let him be aware that she knows anything—she would have to play the fool.

If Cyrus was really Snake Eyes where was the gold? A horrible realization hit her like a bag of bricks in the stomach. The money for the ranch, her ranch, had been stolen from the Soldiers of the Ninth Cavalry. The soldiers and their families depended on that money. She recalled Clarisse and the sergeant, some of that money belonged to him, and their dreams depended on that.

Cyrus had lied to her. He really had lost all of his money gambling. The stolen money from the stagecoach robbery was the only way he would've been able to buy her that new engagement ring, and eventually the ranch. She felt sick to her stomach.

What else had he kept from her, if he had hidden a secret this big? She couldn't think about that now. She had to find the money without him knowing about it. She didn't care about the ranch anymore. It would haunt her all her life if her dream was made possible because it fed upon the hard work and dreams of others. It wasn't right.

# Chapter XXXIV

Billy woke up the next morning with a crick in his spine. The military cots they were provided with just weren't up to par when it came to sleeping in comfort. He looked over his shoulder, to his surprise his tent-mate was not snoring, nor even present. Billy rubbed his eyes and put his hat on and walked out of the tent. Jack was crouching outside fiddling with a handful of dirt. He knew what was on Jack's mind.

"Asked her yet?" Billy said.

"Nope, she's resting up at the fort."

"You still gonna do it?"

"I reckon I will," Jack said, "Just gotta work out a few kinks… ain't got no money and I ain't got no horse. How the hell can I expect her to go with me to Santa Fe when I can't even get there myself? I gotta find the Buffalo Soldiers' money and the bastard who stole it, collect my reward or there ain't no hope."

Billy stood there for a moment with his hands on his hips.

"I tell you what," he said, "now that I got my old mare back you can ride my Apache horse."

Jack turned his head to face him, "That's mighty generous of you."

"Now let's go find those thieving sons of bitches." Billy said.

"Where do you reckon we start?" Jack said to get Billy to recall the events of the stagecoach robbery.

Billy remembered that they wore bandannas over their faces. The thing that stood out the most to him was that Snake Eyes ordered his men not to steal from the passengers. Why did he do that? In all the stories of stagecoach robberies he had ever heard the bandits demanded personal valuables as well as whatever was in the lockbox. No one ever got out without losing something.

Snake Eyes also had an unusual accent, like a dandy who had gone out West. Billy couldn't figure it. Where could a dude like that be? He wouldn't have to rob if he was a respectable citizen with a ranching establishment, so he wouldn't be on the outskirts of town. There was only one other place he could be, in the heart of San Angelo. The whole place from what he'd seen was populated by cowboys, gamblers, drunkards and thieves. He thought about the other eyewitnesses, the passengers, present during the stagecoach robbery. Violet and Maybelle were facing the robbers and most importantly Snake Eyes when it all happened. Also there was himself, the old man and Jimbo on the top of the stagecoach.

Billy thought about going up to the fort to question Maybelle who was still resting up there. It was so soon after the rescue from the Comanche that Billy decided to give it some time. Also, the home of her sister and brother-in-law which she had been staying had been burnt beyond saving.

He thought of Violet. She had seen the robbers with her sharp eyes. Would it be too much of a risk to ask her? If he was seen with her by Edmund Forrester, her life could be at risk. If he and Jack went into town together he would have an extra gun for protection. Perhaps Jack could speak with Violet and ask her if she knew or heard anything of Snake Eyes's whereabouts. That way she wouldn't be seen with Billy, and she'd stay safe. If you find the leader, you find them all.

"We'll start looking in San Angelo today." Billy said.

\* \* \*

Violet had to meet for lunch with Cyrus at noon. That gave her at least four hours to find the gold. What was she doing? What kind of mess had she gotten herself into? She wished that her mother was still alive, and here with her to provide some much needed advice.

Where could Cyrus have put the money? She heard one man call him Snake Eyes, but she couldn't fully believe it until she held those government minted US gold coins in her hands.

The obvious place to check would be his hotel room. If he was there, she could just say that she wanted to visit him, and hopefully he would believe her. The suspicion crept up on her that Cyrus may have recognized her when he was disguised as Snake Eyes while robbing the stagecoach. She walked out of the shop and back to the DeWitt hotel. She knocked on his door, just in case he might be home. No one answered. The door was unlocked so she let herself in. That was the first sign that the gold wasn't there. She looked anyway. Perhaps Cyrus had enough gumption to leave it unprotected, because he expected no one to be looking for it. She looked in all the usual places one would hide things: under the brass bed, the mattress, the behind the desk, under his pillow, in his dresser drawers.

When she opened the first drawer she found something unusual, but it wasn't the gold. It was a bright purple women's garter. She had never owned an item so fancy. She dropped it in disgust as she realized that it must belong to Jeannine. So she had told the truth that night outside the Painted Parrot. Violet backed away and a feeling of nausea hit her deep in her stomach. Jeannine might have told her the truth that night, but Violet didn't regret punching her. That impertinent tart deserved it.

She searched the rest of the drawers, nothing. She was careful to put everything back as she originally found it, as not to raise suspicion—even the garter.

It was a dead end. As she folded a pair of black suit trousers back to their original shape, a single coin fell out of one of the pockets with a clink on the hardwood floor. It glimmered gold. She picked it up and examined it. She ran the tips of her fingers over the shielded eagle and the tiny detail of stars and rays on the reverse, written on the bottom was Twenty D. She turned it over, on the obverse was a woman with the word liberty on her crown that sat above her flowing locks, it was dated 1869. There wasn't a scratch on it.

That newly minted coin confirmed in her mind the truth that she had been unwilling to see. Cyrus must've kept that one for spending money and since he had so much to go around forgot about it in his trouser pant.

This single coin wasn't enough to convict him. The mint-condition coins were probably floating all around the city now in the bars, gambling houses, and brothels. Unless she found his entire share it wouldn't do her any good. He said that he had enough money for the ranch, so it had to be somewhere mostly intact. Just *where* was the problem. The hair on the back of her neck stood up and she decided to leave his room as soon as possible before he discovered her there. She turned around to make sure everything was left as she found it, and bounded out.

Violet's head was spinning and she felt dizzy. She wanted to get back to the stable to do something about it, to tell Billy, but she couldn't. She groped her way down the spinning hallway and into her room. She breathed rapidly as she realized she only had a few more hours to reach Billy and tell him the news about Cyrus.

She almost couldn't believe her own thoughts. Cyrus robbed the stagecoach.

She shook her head as the moments from the stable seemed to creep back into her mind. How could she betray Cyrus, the one she had loved so long? All of the sweet talk, every 'darling', every 'dearest' was an act. She had to face it. Cyrus didn't love her anymore, at least not how she recognized love. Perhaps he was hanging onto the dying ember of the fire, but it could never be love again—after it all, after Jeannine and the robbery and the lies.

Though she wanted to make the right decision and tell the Buffalo Soldiers where they could find their man, but her body wouldn't move. She had loved Cyrus with every fiber of her being and now that same body was resisting her. The room continued to spin as her thoughts became more confusing. She had never felt like this before in her life, so out of control of her own body, her own feelings, her own sense of right, wrong, and duty. She took a deep breath and the room began to spin less and her thoughts became clearer.

She knew she had to tell Billy, but how? He could be anywhere by now. She would start in the most logical place, Fort Concho. If he was not there she'd have to search the town itself without arousing suspicion from Cyrus and his many friends. Still, she couldn't grasp what she was doing. She had to turn Cyrus in—it was the right thing to do. She mustered up her strength, wiped the beads of sweat from her forehead, grabbed her gun belt and slung it around her waist.

If Cyrus caught her there she hoped that it would look like she was performing a normal activity—just riding her new horse. Her legs felt like rubber as she walked down the street and the slight hill leading up to the stable. She felt that at any moment she would lose her balance, and she was amazed that her legs could carry her at all. As she approached the red stallion in the dusty stall it didn't twitch or neigh nervously like before.

She remembered when Billy had told her to stay with Cyrus. Those three words made her shudder now when she thought of them. The situation had changed. She could only hope that she and Billy would not be seen together, so that Edmund Forrester would not make the connection.

She walked the horse out of the stable. When the sun hit her face she saw Cyrus. He was holding the three bags she had hidden underneath the bush.

"You forgot these." he said.

"What do you mean? I never had those." she said.

"Stop it muffin—you were never a good liar."

Violet tried to continue the charade as she gripped the reins tighter. "I don't what you're talking ab—"

"You know what I'm talking about. I talked to the Veck's clerk. He said you purchased a bag of apples, oats, and carrots, respectively. And I happened to find them under that little bush…" Cyrus made a mocking smile, "I wonder why you hid them there in such a hurry. Did you not want someone to know you had been there?"

Violet's eyes were as wide as saucers, and she had one hand on the saddle horn but stared at him dumbstruck. She didn't know what to say or do. Should she admit to the truth?

"You know who I am. Why not say it?" he said.

"Cyrus—" she tried to reason with him.

"Don't call me Cyrus, call me what you know me as."

He stepped forward; his green eyes tightly squinted so Violet could no longer see the whites of his eyes.

"You're Snake Eyes." she said quietly, as she looked him the face. She almost didn't believe her own words as they ushered from her mouth.

"Good. Now I can trust you never to tell anyone. Isn't that right dearest? Or were you planning on informing the authorities while out on your morning ride?"

Violet's throat went dry. She put her foot in the stirrup and pulled herself up in the saddle.

"I'm sorry…" she hit the red horse hard with two kicks of her spurs and it galloped out with a wild rage toward the fort.

Cyrus scrambled to find a horse in the stable, and pursued Violet.

The fort loomed ahead like a sentinel on the prairie. How would she tell Sergeant Hopkins once she was there? She could hear the sound of hoofbeats coming up fast behind her. She turned her head back and saw Cyrus pursuing her on a shining black horse. He had always been a good horseman, perhaps even more skilled than she. She prayed that he would not catch up to her and that her new horse would keep speed.

She crashed down into the Concho River, the red stallion still going at full bore. The water rose up the animal's chest. Her boots and riding skirt became saturated as the water climbed up to the saddle. Looking back she could see Cyrus behind her, his horse hesitating as it entered the water. Once she crossed the river she felt the fleeting sense of safety as Cyrus struggled to get control of his mount, but soon he was halfway across.

As her horse rushed toward the fort, it didn't seem like she was getting any closer. It was like a nightmare. Her worst fears were realized,

Cyrus knew.

Paranoia crept up on her. What would he do if he caught up to her? The hoofbeats were growing louder and her red stallion foamed at the mouth. It sprinted fast like lightning and now the other horse like thunder, was catching up to it. Out of the corner of her eye she could see the horse and

Cyrus had almost overtaken her—his arm stretched out.

"What are you doing?" He cried over the sound of the galloping horses.

"I have to tell them." she yelled.

"No you don't," His hand drew closer. "I did this for you."

She didn't want to hear it anymore. She turned her horse sharply to the right just to be rid of him. But the black horse kept pace. Cyrus's hand reached out yet again, she could feel his fingers on the nape of her neck as he grabbed ahold of her collar.

"Let go of me!" she screamed as his horse skidded to a halt, the overextended legs stick straight. She was flung onto his horse and he held her hands behind her back. She watched helplessly as the red stallion ran off into oblivion. "What are you doing, Cyrus?" she asked calmly as the pressure from his clamped hands made her wrists ache.

"I already warned you that I couldn't let you alert the authorities."

"You can let go of me now. I'm not going anywhere."

"Good girl."

He released his iron-like grasp, and the skin around her wrists breathed free. She hated the way he spoke to her, as if she were a child. She had experienced more pain and hardship than he was aware, just to find him. She shook her head in remembrance of all she had sacrificed for someone so devious and heartless. Cyrus quickly turned the horse around back to San Angelo.

"Where are you taking me?" she demanded.

"Back to the hotel, sweetheart."

"Don't call me sweetheart! I know all about you and Jeannine."

"How do you know about that?" Cyrus said through a clenched jaw.

"She told me."

"And you believed her?"

Violet lied, "I had no reason not to."

"She's just a low-down lying hussy."

"I went through your things. I saw her garter." Violet said defiantly.

Cyrus said nothing. They pulled up to the DeWitt hotel. Violet tried to make a run for it, but he grabbed her by the arms.

"Where are you running to, little rabbit?"

She struggled to get free but he soon had both of her wrists in a tight grip behind her back.

"Don't make a scene." he whispered in her ear.

She stared at her gun slung in front of her, and out of reach. Out of the corner of her eye Violet saw someone she recognized, it was the kid from the stagecoach. He was almost hidden behind a wagon. She couldn't even shout out for help.

Cyrus walked her into the hotel lobby and up to his hotel room. He finally let her go with a push when the door was shut. She stumbled and fell to her knees on the floor. This newly discovered anger and betrayal that she felt from Cyrus boiled within her. She got up, turned around and landed a punch on his jaw. She stood there for a moment, slightly shocked at what she had done. Cyrus also stood there stroking it with his hand with a wicked gleam in his eye.

"I was hoping that this encounter wouldn't turn violent, but it's in your nature I suppose."

Violet was even more angry, but she wouldn't let him get to her. So she slowly unclenched her sweating fist.

"Why didn't you let me tell the Buffalo Soldiers?"

Cyrus guffawed, "Are you kidding me? If those brunettes found out I was the one who stole their money I'd get at least ten years in a federal prison. You wouldn't want that for me, would you?"

Violet eyed him with disbelief. "You should have let me do it. They might have made a deal with you, if you were willing to return the money." She swallowed as she thought of the next words she would speak, "What did you expect, Cyrus? That I would just marry you, and that we could live the rest of our lives in peace? I could never do that knowing that the money we had for the ranch was stolen. I don't care what it was for, you couldn't build me a castle from stolen money that I would accept."

"I'm sorry you feel that way," he said, "but the world is a much crueler place than you could ever imagine."

"Only because of people like you, who lie and steal and cheat." Her mouth was running off on her again.

"I did it for you!" he screamed as he threw his hat down, "I thought we could be happy."

"I can't love you Cyrus. Not anymore." She felt only pity for the man she once loved. Tears began to well up in her eyes and she reached for the doorknob. Cyrus blocked the door. "What are you doing?" she implored.

"I know you're going to tell the cavalry. I can't let you do that, Violet."

"Let me leave, Cyrus." she said as she tried to get past his human barricade.

"No, missy."

She reached for the doorknob again, but he grabbed her hand and flung her against the side of the brass bed. The last thing she saw were the baseboards before her vision became fuzzy gray and then black.

\* \* \*

Billy saddled up the Apache horse and Jack followed him into town. They hitched up in front of the DeWitt hotel. Billy was extra cautious, knowing that he had a price on his head. Edmund Forrester could be anywhere, lurking in the shadows of the dark alleyways.

"Hey cowboy," a young voice called.

Billy turned on his heel the boy from the stagecoach was standing in the shadows behind the wagon. For a moment Billy thought that this might be a trap set up by Forrester. Would he stoop so low as to use a kid as bait?

"Howdy Jimbo, what're you doing out here?" Billy asked. Jimbo motioned for him to come closer. The young man had an earnest expression, and Billy couldn't see anyone else near him so he obeyed—his hand hovering over the pistol handle wary of a trap. "What is it?"

"I saw your girl just a few minutes ago—"

"You mean Violet? She ain't my girl, but we need to talk to her. Where is she?"

"That's just it—a tall, dark looking feller forced her into the hotel. Something didn't seem right about it."

Billy's jaw dropped, he knew that was Cyrus by Jimbo's description.

"Thanks kid." Billy turned to Jack. "We need to get to Violet—I think she might be in trouble."

Violet tried to hold her pounding head but the twisting of the rope on her wrists stopped her. She was placed like a sack of flour in the corner of Cyrus's hotel room next to the window. Her ankles were bound as well. Cyrus was sitting on the bed, a gun in his hand.

"Are the restraints really necessary?" she chided.

"You're the one who punched me and was planning on turning me into the authorities."

She moved the drapes of Cyrus's hotel room window with her nose to look outside. Beneath she saw the familiar Apache horse hitched outside of the hotel, and could recognize Jack from his long serape. Cyrus pulled the drapes shut suddenly.

"No peeking." he said.

She hoped with all hopes that Billy was with Jack. Perhaps they were looking for her, to ask her questions about the stagecoach robbery. What other reason could they be at the hotel? Unless they already knew about Cyrus, but that was doubtful. She could hear muffled footsteps of boots coming up the creaky hotel stairway. As they came closer she could hear spurs. Two sets of spurs. There was a faint knock on a door down the hall. Perhaps it was on her hotel room door. She had to do something—it might be her only opportunity of escape.

"Help!" she yelled. She couldn't think of anything else to say.

Cyrus looked at her with fear and rage.

"What the hell are you doing? I should have thought to have you gagged."

She called out again. She could hear the footsteps running down the hall. Cyrus pulled the hammer back on his pistol and aimed for the door. With a pain in her heart Violet realized what she had done—she had lead Billy and Jack into a trap.

A bottom of a boot hit the door and it swung open. A shot was fired from Cyrus's gun. Another shot was fired at Cyrus. He ducked behind the bed. She tried to break free from her bonds, but she couldn't get them loose enough for her to slip through. Billy entered the room, crouched down. He crawled over to Violet and cut the rope from her feet and hands with his Bowie knife. Cyrus was too distracted avoiding fire from Jack to see the intruder. Billy and Violet crawled out of room on their hands and knees to avoid the crossfire. Jack kept returning fire as Billy rushed her down the stairs and out of the hotel. Jack followed closely behind. They finally made it out into the street.

"Are you alright?" Billy asked as he held her face with both hands.

"I'm fine. Thanks for coming for me,"

"We better get going. He's madder than a hornet." Jack said as he ran from the swinging hotel doors out onto the street. "Billy, he's the one." Violet began, "He's Snake Eyes, I tried to tell—"

Cyrus stormed out the doors, looking wilder and more venomous than a rattlesnake. Violet instinctively went for her gun, but all she grabbed at was air. Of course Cyrus would've taken it while she was knocked out. Billy stood in front of her, his back turned to Cyrus. Jack overheard what Violet had said, turning around and pointing his gun at a very frazzled, very wild Cyrus.

"Alright sir. We know who you are. You can just drop that gun and we won't have any more trouble." Jack said.

Cyrus stood there half crouched, sweat glistened off his tanned forehead, he had the look of a cornered coyote. Billy was still standing in front of Violet with his pistol drawn toward Cyrus.

"We speak for the federal government. You're a wanted man, Cyrus." Billy said, adding to Jack's statement, "Put the gun down."

"Please Cyrus." Violet pleaded one last time as she stepped aside from Billy for a moment to show her face.

Cyrus smiled his wolf-like grin and slowly lowered the gun to the dirt. "I guess I have no choice."

His hand hovered a little too long over the pistol once it was lying in the street.

"Hands to the sky, pardner!" Billy ordered.

Cyrus obeyed, still wearing that sardonic smile on his face and kicked the gun away, it slid toward Billy.

"You have me gentlemen. There was no sense in resisting." he said it coolly, as if he had kept his head the entire time.

Jack came from the side and bound his hands.

"Let's get a move on." Jack said as he led Cyrus to his horse, "Any funny business and I ain't ashamed to put a bullet in your back."

Violet watched, stone-faced. Only this morning she had not known that Cyrus was Snake Eyes. Not only that he had kidnapped her and tried to kill two of her friends. His steely green eyes seemed to penetrate her as he was led to Jack's horse. She didn't know what to do or say so she just stood and watched. How could someone she had loved so dearly betray her so? She didn't understand it. A shred of guilt pervaded her. She almost felt like she should apologize to Cyrus, but there was no reason to. He had done more wrong to her, than she ever did to him. He had done the deed and now it was time for him to pay for it. Justice would be served. It came as so much of a shock to her she could scarcely believe it.

Billy put his hands on her shoulders. "I have to go now. Will you be alright?" His tender eyes intimated to the situation with Cyrus.

"I'll be fine." she replied, "Go."

Billy left with Jack, and a captive Cyrus in tow. Jack mumbled something to Billy. His blue eyes stayed on her until they were out of sight.

Violet stood alone in the street as she watched the two men with their prisoner, who just an hour before was her fiancé. Cyrus was gone. He would be tried and convicted for armed robbery. They might even add kidnapping and evading a federal officer to the list. His sentence would be steep, at least ten years. The man that she had loved, and her future with him was gone forever. She was grateful she knew the truth. She would rather spend her life alone than love someone who had lied to her and perhaps never truly loved her. She was not only grateful, but in fact glad. Her watery eyes looked up at the sky so bold and beautiful in its vastness. The sun shone high, and its rays spread out above the rambling prairie. Her life would never be the same again.

# Chapter XXXV

When the morning was new and the dew still on the ground Violet rode out to Fort Concho for the last time. Sergeant Hopkins greeted her at the entrance.

"Pleasure to formally meet you, ma'am." he tipped his hat, "I want to thank you personally for your help in returning the money. I heard you suffered more than a woman should."

"I'm glad I could have been of assistance, it would have stayed on my conscious the rest of my life if I had stayed quiet." she said, "I do have a favor to ask you. May I see the prisoner?"

"Certainly," the sergeant said as he led her to a small jail cell. "This is where we're keeping him until he can stand trial in a court of law." Cyrus sat in the corner on a floor lined with straw. "I'll leave you two alone."

Cyrus looked up at her with surprise in his eyes. Defeat and anguish were written all over his face, it was as if he aged ten years.

"What are you doing here?" he said.

"I wanted to see how you were—how you were being treated."

"Just dandy,"

Violet looked over at the ground for a moment. "I'm not sure what to say…"

"Then say nothing."

Her eyebrows lowered, "No, I do know what I'm going to say. I'm sorry. I'm sorry that you chose to do the things you did. I'm sorry that I ever trusted you. I'm sorry that you didn't love me as much as I loved you. I'm sorry that you were too much of a coward to tell me the truth. I'm sorry that you chose to throw away our life together. I'm sorry."

Cyrus glanced up at her, with the look of a frightened dog. He said nothing.

"Goodbye Cyrus, I hope you're happy with Jeannine." she turned around added with an impish smile, "Oh, sorry about her nose."

Violet packed her things. Her remaining items were spread out on the quilt of her hotel bed. Many were tattered and damaged beyond repair. She had to visit Cyrus's old room to retrieve her ivory-handled gun, it had been lying there on the bed. She looked over her items with fondness, and each seemed to recall memories. She didn't know where she would go. Perhaps back home to Missouri. Wherever she went, she didn't care. She was content to go wherever her life path took her.

She unloaded her revolver and took it apart carefully. She began to clean each piece with precision and delicacy, savoring the moment. Wherever she was to go she needed a horse, and didn't have enough left of her belongings to sell or barter for one. Technically she already had a horse, though it might have joined in with a herd of its wild mustang cousins.

She looked out the window. Below, she could see the familiar hide of that red horse that had escaped so fearfully just the other day, it looked as though it had just wandered back into town. She ran down the hotel stairs, hoping to retrieve it before someone else falsely claimed it as their own. She bounded out the doors. As she turned she saw someone she did not expect. Billy stood there holding both the reins of her red horse and that of his quarter horse. He tipped his hat.

"What are you doing here?" Violet asked. She knew he shouldn't be in town, Forrester was looking for him.

"I had to bring your horse back. Saw him wandering outside of the fort looking awful lonesome." Billy smiled broadly, "Would you like to go for a ride?"

"Of course," she said as she petted the stallion's neck. They both got on their steeds and rode off into the wild prairie. Once they were away from the town, Violet felt happy for the first time in a long time. The breeze ran through her hair and she outstretched her arms as the stallion went on a full gallop. She felt completely free and happy like a hawk on the wind.

As she rode her horse with arms outstretched Billy watched her smile broadly, the first time he had ever really seen her smile. It was one of the most beautiful things he had ever seen.

She took the reins again and Billy led her to the bank of the river where the cypress and oak trees grew up tall and strong. He helped her off her horse and she landed right next to him. He was so close she couldn't help but throw her arms around him. It was as good as a thank you. His embrace was so strong and warm and she wished she could live there forever. As she withdrew, she realized she didn't want to leave, and at that moment he kissed her. It was a kiss filled with passion and desperation, a love that had been quiet for so long was finally being expressed. It was different than that kiss with Cyrus, this one was so warm and true that it almost scared her, she never knew that a kiss could make her feel so whole. She stepped back, quite in awe of what had happened.

Billy took her by the hand and led her down to the bank of the river.

"I've been meaning to tell you something for a long while, but hadn't yet got the chance," Billy said as his eyes gazed out beyond the river. "Seeing as you had been promised to another man." He took a deep breath. "I've loved you Violet, ever since I saw you in the saloon and you pistol-whipped Smith in the back of the head." He laughed. His blue eyes looked thoughtful and seemed to match the color of the sky, and the brilliance of the sun. "I suppose it was rather a selfish thing for me to help you find Cyrus, because I wanted to get to know you... Anyway, I reckon you're the most remarkable woman I ever had the pleasure of acquainting." He looked her in the eyes and he stuttered, "What I mean to say is, Violet... I want to marry you."

He waited for a response as Violet watched the humble cowboy propose with her studied quietude. She knew that Billy had feelings for her, but she was unaware of their actual intensity until now. Her heart which had once tortured her by tugging it in two directions was numb. She had no idea what to say to the young man whom she had loved but could not admit to it just days earlier. Part of her was happy and ready to throw her arms around him and accept the love he so openly offered. The other part wanted to ride off into unknown expanses. She was confused, and though the ingenuous cowboy expressed true feelings of love she was not ready to accept them just yet. But in her heart of hearts she knew where she belonged.

He wondered what was taking her so long to answer him. From her silence he surmised that she was upset because he made no mention of his precarious situation. He continued, "I know I'm asking much, to expect you to take a wanted man. But now that I have the reward money, we can get out of San Angelo. I'll take care of Forrester and the Smiths myself. I know we can make it work. I'll do anything to protect you, Violet. I'd die for you." He spoke so earnestly it tore her heart apart.

"Billy, I believe you." As a smile lit up his face she continued, "But I can't marry you... not just yet. It's something I can't explain, and something I don't quite understand myself." She shook her head-- it was all coming out a jumbled mess. "I just need some time."

Billy put his boot heel up on a rock. He nodded once and looked over the horizon to the distant blue ranges. "I get you, Violet. I'll wait as long as you want me to before I marry you. But I will marry you." He looked up at her and smiled his half-grin.

Violet smiled back. "Until later Billy." She mounted her horse and rode back toward town.

After a few hundred feet she stopped her horse and looked back. He was still standing there at the river bank, skipping a stone across the water.

What was the use in waiting? She knew that Cyrus was a bad man and that he probably never truly loved her. Now she finds out that a brave, loyal, and honorable young man wants to marry her. And the truth was, she loved him back. What was the harm in accepting that love? She knew that after Cyrus betrayed her that Billy wouldn't force the issue of marriage. He might wait forever if she let him. But she couldn't do that to him; he deserved better than that. She loved him and wanted him to be happy, and she offered the best hope for his happiness.

She bit her lip, and looked back again at that man. That man who when she first met him she underestimated him and thought of as just a boy, when in reality he was more of a man than Cyrus. Cyrus, who had been revered by her somewhat as a holy figure, but when it came down to the truth, he fell short. Cyrus was a coward.

Billy was the bravest man she had ever met. She turned her horse around, and rode back to Billy's side. He stared at her in jubilant surprise.

"I knew you'd come back, you stubborn woman." Billy said. He embraced her, and held her close to him. He lifted her up as if they were crossing the threshold as husband and wife, and he spun her around. The sound of their laughter rang together in harmony.